PENGUIN BOOKS
ST AGNES' STAND

Thomas Eidson is the president and chief executive officer of a large communications firm. His grandparents lived in Oklahoma Territory, Kansas, and Southern Colorado, and it is out of oral family histories and storytelling that *St Agnes' Stand* grew.

St Agnes' Stand was shortlisted for the 1994 *Sunday Express* Book of the Year Award.

D1152403

St Agnes' Stand

THOMAS EIDSON

PENGUIN BOOKS

PENGUIN BOOKS

Published by the Penguin Group
Penguin Books Ltd, 27 Wrights Lane, London W8 5TZ, England
Penguin Books USA Inc., 375 Hudson Street, New York, New York 10014, USA
Penguin Books Australia Ltd, Ringwood, Victoria, Australia
Penguin Books Canada Ltd, 10 Alcorn Avenue, Toronto, Ontario, Canada M4V 3B2
Penguin Books (NZ) Ltd, 182–190 Wairau Road, Auckland 10, New Zealand

Penguin Books Ltd, Registered Offices: Harmondsworth, Middlesex, England

First published by Michael Joseph 1994
Published in Penguin Books 1995
7 9 10 8 6

Printed in England by Clays Ltd, St Ives plc

For my children
Samantha, Elizabeth and John
"Have I ever told you. . . ?"

Day One...

_____

He was hurt and riding cautiously. Thoughts not quite grasped made him uneasy, and he listened for an errant sound in the hot wind. His eyes were narrowed – searching for a broken leaf, a freshly turned rock, anything from which he could make some sense of his vague uneasiness. Nothing. The desert seemed right, but wasn't somehow. He turned in the saddle and looked behind him. A tumbleweed was bouncing in front of wild assaults from the wind. But the trail was empty. He turned back and sat, listening.

Over six feet and carrying two hundred pounds, Nat Swanson didn't disturb easy, but this morning he was edgy. His hat brim was pulled low, casting his face in shadow. The intense heat and the wind were playing with the air, making it warp and shimmer over the land. He forced himself to peer through it, knowing he wouldn't get a second chance if he missed a sheen off sweating skin or the straight line of a gun barrel among branches.

As his mule climbed, he slowly reached his hands back and pulled black shoulder-length hair out of the way behind his head, securing it with a piece of silk ribbon. Caught in this way, the hair revealed the finely shaped features of his weathered profile. His skin was a dark copper colour and sun lines etched deep into the corners of his eyes and mouth gave his face the look of cracked rock when he smiled.

Without much motion, he slipped the leather thong off the hammer of the pistol hanging at his side, easing the weapon halfway up the holster to clear it, then settling it back down again. The sheer cold weight of it felt comforting.

He had been running for a week, and he was light on sleep and heavy on dust and too ready for trouble. He'd killed a man in a West Texas town he'd forgotten the name of – over a woman whose name he'd never known. He hadn't wanted the woman or the killing. Nor had he wanted the hole in his thigh. What he did want was to get to California, and that's where he was headed. Buttoned in his shirt pocket was a deed for a Santa Barbara ranch. Perhaps a younger man would have run longer and harder before turning to fight and maybe die; but Nat Swanson was thirty-five years that summer, old for the trail, and he had run as far as he was going to run.

A covey of mearns quail flushed near the ridge top and glided down the bright mountain air, disappearing in a thick stand of manzanita to his left. He reined the mule in and sat watching. The animal stood with its ears tilted back, then switched them forward and listened up the trail. The mule was desert-bred stock, and Swanson knew it sensed the danger as well as he. The uneasy feeling came over him strong again, and he blew out his nostrils to clear them and then breathed in, scenting the wind. Nothing. But there *was* something. Mearns quail didn't flush easy in high winds.

4

It was early morning and he was perched halfway up a hardscrabble New Mexico hillside, following a deer path that stayed comfortably below the crestline where a larger pack trail ran. It was habit with him never to ride main trails or ridge lines even in the best of times, and this morning, with three riders tracking him, he wasn't about to start breaking the habit.

He ran facts over in his mind. It didn't figure that the men who had chased him across miles of hot desert on bad water had magically managed to get ahead of him. Even if they could have pushed their animals that hard, which he plain doubted, they couldn't have guessed which arroyo he would take into the high mountains. No man was that lucky. There was no sense to it, and he was a man who liked things to make sense.

A sound from behind told Swanson the dog had worked its way up through the brush of the mountain. He looked over his shoulder at it sitting on its thin haunches, its eyes and ears fixed on the trail ahead; at least they weren't coming at his back. He let the dog take a blow. It stood some six hands at the shoulders, deep-chested, maybe ninety pounds, narrow at the hips. Nature had left its tail long for balance, and somebody else had spiked its ears so they couldn't be torn off in a fight. Great patches of bare skin showed on its haunches and shoulders where its thin hair had been worn off in sleep against the hard desert. It was as formidable a beast as it was ugly; a fierce and violent mongrel, able to take a man down and able to kill.

Five years before, the dog had thrown in with him in Arizona, swinging silently in behind his mule one sundown in a high mountain meadow a hundred miles from anywhere or anyone. That's all he knew about it, excepting it was clean, didn't beg, wasn't friendly and didn't make noise; those were things he understood and respected. It had bitten him once, and he had thought of shooting it more times than that.

When the dog was rested, he waved it ahead. It trotted past the mule and began to zigzag in the brush on both sides of the trail. Five yards from the hilltop, it froze. Swanson watched it for a few seconds and then swung painfully down, keeping his right hand free. When he reached the ground he pulled a leather pouch from behind the cantle of his saddle and slung it under his arm; then he loosened the straps holding a crossbow in place, listening hard as he worked, and slipped the weapon across his back. He checked the cylinder on his pistol and started up the trail.

Even hurt, he was deceptively light on his feet. He wore soft, mule-eared boots and moved with a grace and power that told of years not spent in a saddle but on foot in mountains like these. His buckskin leggings and his four-button blue flannel shirt were soft and noiseless as he walked. He knew the dog had a scent but the wind kept it confused, and he watched it now turning and sticking its nose up, then turning again. He continued climbing.

The dog was nowhere in sight as Swanson eased over the crest of the trail. The pain was bad in his leg. He lay still for a long time in a patch of dried hopsage and listened to the hills. No sound. The morning sun burned into him. He squinted his eyes and searched for movement. The wind had died. Just heat and dust and gravel. The flies and gnats hadn't started in yet. The air felt pure and clean and hot. He crawled forward until he was

6

overlooking a wide canyon that fell sharply away from where he lay concealed. At the bottom he could see a rocky flat and a dry river bed; a line of stunted tamarisk trees, parched and almost leafless, bordered the waterless course of the river. Nothing looked alive.

He had not spotted them before he heard the popping of a musket. Seconds later, there was a louder, sharper bark from what sounded like a Hawken. He squinted and searched the canyon until he located the white smoke drifting in the air, and after a few minutes more of searching he saw the Indian who had fired the musket. Ten minutes later, he had marked the positions of thirty Apaches, and seen their prey.

Two freight wagons lay overturned in a V against a cliff at the edge of a narrow road. Swanson pulled a telescope from the leather pouch and scanned them. The remains of a water barrel indicated the standoff would be short, Hawken or not. The wood looked dry. But maybe whoever was behind the wagons still had water. For their sake, he hoped so.

He glassed the road again. It was going to be a game with only one end: the freighters were eventually going to go crazy from the heat, the thirst, the fear . . . and one night they were going to try and escape. They wouldn't make it.

He gave them three days, maybe. They were probably Mexicans; two to a wagon and armed with muzzle loaders and single-ball pistols. The Hawken might mean their cargo was valuable. It didn't matter. No one would come to help them. They knew that. They knew the Apache. Their people had brutalized one another from time out of mind. They were *muerto*. The best they could hope was not to be taken alive. He couldn't help them.

He held the telescope on some rocks near one of the wagons. The Indians had started a landslide in an attempt to knock the closest dray off the road, but it had missed. The stones lay in a mass higher than the wagons. The Apaches had seen this and two stood behind the rocks motioning for a third to climb up and take a shot.

Swanson focused the scope on this Indian. He was wearing a red shirt strapped at the waist with a leather belt, a white breechcloth, bare legged with deerskin boots. He looked no more than sixteen, but from the easy way he carried the musket in the crook of his arm, the way he strode confidently up the rocky slope, it was obvious this was their marksman.

Swanson studied him closely: the respect he was being shown by the others, his arrogance, and the comfortable manner in which he handled the weapon said he knew how to shoot. With just yards separating the mound of rocks from the wagons, he was going to give the people behind the wagons jessy; it would be like plunking thirsty horses at a water hole.

Swanson didn't love Mexicans, but he liked them somewhat better than a stacked deck. Even so, he figured it wasn't his funeral. He was calculating on pulling back and staying out of the fight, when he saw the Indian in the red shirt, a cock-of-the-walk grin on his poxed face, standing on the road in clear view of the wagons, urinating; daring the trapped Mexicans to do something. He wasn't twenty feet from the closest wagon. It seemed incredible. Swanson waited for the Hawken to bark; waited for the pissing Apache to fly backwards, his chest blown open. Nothing happened.

He couldn't figure it; why don't they just shoot the

sonofabitch, he wondered. Like jack rabbits cornered by the dog, they must be frozen with fear. That, or they'd already killed themselves. He had heard of that happening, though he didn't know whether to believe it or not; it seemed impossible an armed man would shoot himself rather than die fighting. But long ago he had learned there was no figuring fear in man or beast.

Still, this act of pissing at men who were going to die, men cornered and outnumbered and who didn't have much of a fighting chance left, men who had maybe just a little bit of dignity left inside their pinched up guts, didn't set well with him. Fact of the matter, while Nat Swanson was slow to anger, this made it for him.

He limped half-crouched down a ridge top to some boulders and squatted behind them, tightening the bloody bandana on his thigh, groaning quietly from the pain. Then he pulled the crossbow off his back, his hands moving over the coffee-coloured wood with familiarity bred over a lifetime. It had been his grandfather's. Swanson knew the hearth stories – the old man had used it to poach deer and boar off the great English estates around Kent in the late 1700s. It must have been a wonderfully efficient weapon for that purpose: powerful, accurate, silent as soft wind through spring leaves.

He placed the butt on his stomach and, grasping the slack string in both hands, yanked back hard, grunting at the hurt in his leg, bending the short metal wings until the string caught in the trigger lock; then he notched a bolt snugly in place and rose slowly over a waist-high boulder, resting the weapon on the stone. He guessed the range, sighted a fraction high, and pulled his breath in. No wind. The Indian was atop the boulders now, making a show of sighting his musket on the two wagons. Swanson let his breath out, then held it and pulled softly. There was no recoil, no sound to speak of, only a soft *twang* as the string slammed forward.

For a fleeting moment, he glimpsed the white fletching arcing through the bright morning sunlight, then he lost it in the shadows of the cliff. One second. Two seconds. Suddenly the Apache's head smashed against the rocks, the body sliding limply to the roadway. It had been a clean kill.

The two Indians who had beckoned the younger brave were crouching against the side of the cliff, searching for who or what had slain their comrade so efficiently, so silently. The heavy one lunged from the wall and yanked up the dead man's arms, dragging the body quickly down the rocky slope, while the second one scrambled after the precious musket. They had no idea where the bolt had come from and that would keep them from climbing the boulders for another shot, for a time.

When it was safe, Swanson studied the wagons again through the telescope, curious. The Indians were still fanned on the slope, but they looked more alert and less confident. He brought the circular field of the lens to play on the wagons and wondered again if there was anyone still alive behind them. There was no movement, but that didn't prove anything; a man would be a damn fool to show himself with Apaches watching. But if they were alive, why hadn't they killed the pissing Apache?

He was moving the circle of glass slowly along the space between the bottom of the wagons and the ground, trying to catch a movement of some kind, when he saw her. He couldn't believe his eyes. A woman's face, not pretty, not young, but a woman, nevertheless, stared out directly at him from the gap between the two wagons, staring as if she were looking straight into his eyes. Then she was gone. Swanson searched the area where he had seen her for another hour, but she never reappeared.

It was blisteringly hot where he hid among the rocks; the gnats had retreated but the flies had taken their place and they were driving him crazy, and he was getting a little wild for water because he'd bled a good deal from the wound. It didn't take much for him to make up his mind to pull out. He just did it. He'd done all he could for the people in the wagons. He had bought them precious time. He was surprised and sorry there was a woman involved, but there wasn't a single logical thing he could do to save her.

He struggled to his knees and put the telescope on the wagons one last time. She wasn't to be seen, but he knew she was there; her face seemed oddly burned into his memory somehow. He guessed it was the surprise of seeing her in the first place, which caused her face to keep flashing in his thoughts. Getting her out would be impossible. Only a fool would try. He was no fool.

The mule was where he had left it. When he had finished restrapping the crossbow and the leather pouch to the saddle, he stood a while, listening for danger and sipping from his canteen, figuring his options. His biggest concern now was the three men behind him. Having lost half the day, they had to be close; and they too would take the road to Fort Rucker, since it was the only place in a hundred miles for fresh horses and supplies.

If he were smart, he would strike west along the Gila River into Arizona Territory; with a little luck, he could make it and the Texans weren't likely to follow him deep into Apacheria. After a week of trying to lose them over hard rock desert and shifting sand that didn't leave much trail sign, and failing to do so, he knew the three men tracking him weren't new at this game, and they certainly weren't fools. They wouldn't want anything to do with the Apache if they could avoid it; not even to avenge the death of a friend.

The Gila was his best chance and quickest route to California; but as he stood there next to his mule, he knew he couldn't take it. Not right off, anyhow. First, he would head for Fort Rucker; he owed the woman at the wagons that one chance. He didn't owe her his life, however, and he promised himself he would turn west the first time his pursuers broke out between him and the fort. Having scouted for the army, he'd take no chance some second-jack cavalry officer would side with the dead man's friends and turn him over to be hung. His mind made up, he didn't expect to have his hand forced quite as soon as it was.

The dog had rejoined him on a trail leading down out of the arroyo, and after he had given it water he had looked up and spotted his pursuers crossing a ridge top half a mile ahead. The sun was behind Swanson and there was little chance the men would see any reflection off the glass, so he stood and put the telescope on them.

They were outfitted and looked like typical Texans, lean and tough, strapped with the new Walker Colt pistols that were making their way into the territory and carrying a selection of different rifles under their legs. One rode a big, high-stepping pinto with a broken tail and a nice singlefoot. It was an animal he might have traded the mule for, and he watched it admiringly. The men's faces were shadowed by large hats, and he couldn't see them; but the way they rode, letting their horses pick the trail, taking care to lean forward over the necks of their mounts whenever they climbed to go easy on the beasts' kidneys, he understood them. And, under different circumstances, he would probably get along with these men. But the circumstances weren't different; he had killed a friend of theirs and now they aimed to kill him, so he waited until they disappeared into a chaparral-filled arroyo, then he mounted and struck west towards the Gila.

The Apaches had won; the woman had lost. It was that simple. There was nothing he could do about it.

He had been riding for half an hour, checking his backtrail periodically, when he came over a bluff and saw the cloth. The sharp colours against the dull taupe hues of the hills seemed to physically slap at his senses. Hundreds of feet of brightly coloured calico cloth were strewn in all directions over the tops of the brush at the bottom of the small valley. Some Apache braves had had fine fun on horseback.

Out the corner of one eye, he saw a thin trail of smoke threading its way into the sky, rising from what appeared to be a third wagon that had broken through the ambush and made it this far. His muscles tensed and a searing pain shot up from the gash in his leg. The dog was standing a few feet in front of the mule, its hair rising in a stiff ridge down the length of its back.

He pulled his pistol and checked the cylinder, then waved the dog into the valley. The air around him was bright and cheerful, filled with the sounds of water and birds. After a quarter hour, the dog returned and flopped down on the trail. He was soaked and satisfied looking and Swanson knew he'd been swimming. He tightened the bandage on his leg and swung down. He had stiffened up, but fortunately the leg had mostly stopped bleeding. Quietly, he worked his way down the slope.

The freight driver had been dead for at least two days and what was left of his head was blackening in a repulsive mass in the heat. Swanson kicked a turkey vulture off the corpse. The bird's ugly bald head and neck were glistening with grease and blood and it was too heavy to fly. It stood off a few yards, its wings outstretched and its mouth open, hissing at Swanson.

The man had been buried to his neck in the soft sand a few yards from the wagon, but not before his privates had been cut off and stuffed in his mouth. His face had been brutally disfigured; his eyelids, nose and ears cut off, an eye gouged out with a stick. Then he'd been used for target practice with lances and arrows. It had probably been over in half an hour, and made him the lucky one. They had taken longer with the woman. Her white skin looked obscene in the sunlight, and Swanson covered her with a black robe he found in the dirt near the wagon.

He had no time to bury them; the Apaches would be back for the cloth and the other goods in the wagon. After taking a long drink and filling his canteens and a deerskin bag, he soaked his head in the clear pool of water, cleaned his wound, and then let the mule drink his full.

He rode through half the night, putting good distance between him and the valley. Five hours before dawn, he made a cold camp in thick mesquite. He hobbled the mule and unsaddled it, drying the animal's back carefully with a cloth; then he turned the blanket over to the dry side and resaddled, half tightening the cinch so that he could still mount if attacked. He cocked the crossbow and slipped a bolt into the firing groove, then he threw a tarp on the ground and lay down in what was still hundred-degree heat and tried to sleep. The feeling of the deed crinkling in his pocket was good.

Sister St Agnes had been praying in the dark for over two hours; she held the crucifix her mother had given her forty-seven years before, on the day she had taken her solemn vows. She had turned twenty that day. The memory flooded in. She could see it vividly: snow had fallen in New York City and her mother and two younger brothers, Matthew and Timothy, had looked so cold and alone standing outside the convent of the Sisters of Charity where she had spent her novitiate, shaking in their winter coats, while she in contrast had felt so warm inside, so at peace. She had known then God was real; He lived. It had been that simple for her. That feeling of peace had never left her; not even now, on this dark, hot night with the shadows of death so near, was she without the peace.

Even so, she was deeply troubled. She rubbed the crucifix gently in her fingers, the way she always did when she needed a special prayer answered. And on this night, in this black and lonely place, hundreds of miles from succour and safety, she needed a very special prayer answered; not for herself, she thought. She was ready to join her Lord. Her prayers, as usual, were simple and were for others. She had two this night and she had been repeating them in different ways over and over again.

The first prayer was for Sister Ruth. She had not made it to safety. Sister St Agnes had watched a group of Indians overtake the fleeing wagon as it rolled down the road; one had shoved Sister Ruth down when she stood up in the back. Sister St Agnes knew instinctively that Sister Ruth was lost. She had not told the others what she had seen; Sister Ruth was their only hope; they had visions of her and the Mexican driver hurrying toward Santa Fe and help. And as long as she did not have to lie, Sister St Agnes would not destroy their hope.

She closed her eyes tighter and prayed fervently for Sister Ruth's soul; she did not pray for her death. Even though she knew of the things that the Apache did to women captives, her faith would not allow her to pray for death. But she could pray for Sister Ruth to have the strength and the peace of the abiding Almighty, and she did. Then she prayed over and over again for Ruth's precious soul. When she was done, she felt weak and alone. She asked the Saviour to comfort Sister Ruth in her hour of need, and she began to talk quietly to her, the way she had once talked at night in her heart to her own father when she was a novice in the convent. She had been deeply troubled then as well.

She felt a gentle warmth inside at the thought of her father. Sister Ruth and he were similar in so many ways. They were both possessed of great pride; not evil pride as some have, but rather a sense of rightness in their actions and being. Stubborn, too. Sister St Agnes smiled at the thought and her mind drifted effortlessly to her father, now dead, whom she loved so much. A Baptist minister, he had never spoken to her after she had become a Catholic and entered the convent.

She was silent for a few moments, and then in a soft, mothering tone she said, 'Sister Ruth, forget where you are now, forget everything, let go of this world. Let Jesus hold you and comfort you. He's coming for you, Ruth, turn away and run to Him.' She was sobbing softly now, not in sorrow, not in joy, simply in farewell. She was smiling through her tears.

After she had composed herself, Sister St Agnes began her second prayer. She appeared to straighten her small body somewhat and she squeezed the crucifix tightly between the palms of her hands. 'Jesus,' she whispered, her voice intensifying, 'I have never asked for a miracle. I have never deserved one. I've never asked for a thing for myself, though You Yourself, Lord, said: "Ask and it shall be given." I am willing to die in this place if that is Your will . . . but . . .' Her words failed her. She clutched harder at the cross in her hands, and for the first time in her life, she felt herself sweating beneath her habit. She shuddered as if a hand had touched her, and the desert night felt oddly cold and penetrating. 'Dear Saviour Jesus, send one who will deliver the others from this evil.'

Sister St Agnes slept.

Nat Swanson sat bolt upright in his sleep, and yelled. The dog came close to him and stared into his face. He reached a trembling hand out toward it and it growled at him and moved away. Swanson was drenched with sweat and he stood up, shaken. He had never yelled like that before in his life and he didn't like it. He sat down on a rock and tried to piece together what had caused it. He looked at his hands; they were still trembling. It was a beautiful, starry night. The dog came and sat down a distance away and watched him, curious. The moon was three-quarters full and seemed to move among brilliant white clouds.

Swanson knew he had been dreaming. That in itself was strange, since he could not recall having ever dreamed before. But he was certain that he had been dreaming. About what, he didn't know. Except that he knew it had something to do with the woman at the wagons. He had seen her face again – a face surrounded by utter darkness – and he had yelled a yell that felt like it had been trapped inside of him all his days. Swanson shook slightly. He called the dog but the animal only stared at him, its fur up on its back.

Three hours before dawn, Nat Swanson cinched the mule up tight and started on again. He rode chewing on a piece of jerky; he tried to stay alert to the trail and the surrounding hills, but his mind kept drifting back to the wagons and the woman. An hour later, he stopped and sat thinking. He felt oddly chilled. The dog was watching him closely, giving him a wide berth.

He rubbed his eyes; he couldn't shake the memory of her face. She didn't look like anyone he had ever known. She wasn't handsome. She wasn't marrying age. He could no longer remember what his own mother looked like, so she couldn't remind him of her. It didn't make sense. There was a new life waiting for him in California. But now, strangely, it was on the periphery of his thoughts. Try as he would, he couldn't get his mind off the face at the wagons. He just sat there, the mule grazing, the dog watching him.

When dawn came and he was still sitting there, still thinking about her, he turned the mule around and started back to the canyon.

*

He stood glassing the arroyos and ridgebacks, looking for a way he could reach the wagons. There was none that wouldn't get him killed, unless he waited until dark, and by that time, he figured, it would be too late. The Apaches were growing bolder. Nine of them were standing on the road, some behind the rocks, some in plain view of the wagons.

Two young bucks who walked like they had been drinking mescal marched boldly out in front of the wagons, turned and pulled their breechcloths up and then, tauntingly, slapped their buttocks. The Hawken rifle barked again; and, startled, the two darted unceremoniously for cover down the rocky slope, their comrades laughing at them. Swanson shook his head, amazed anyone could miss with a rifle at that distance.

Minutes later, the Apaches were tossing fist-sized rocks over the wagons and yelling taunts. Twice on the wind, he heard their word for whore. This wasn't going to last much longer; soon a brave would get high enough on peyote or mescal, grab a lance and rush the wagons, others would follow, and it would be over.

Unpleasant as it was to think of the woman dying in this way, it gave him an odd idea, one that just might work. As quickly as caution would allow, he mounted and rode the mule into the shadows of a scrub oak that stood alongside the main ridge trail overlooking the canyon. He held the cocked crossbow in his hands as he searched for the two Indians who had been slapping their buttocks at the wagons. He singled them out because they were the most brazen of the band, most eager to be at the victims behind the wagons.

They were standing behind the boulders on the road

now, dancing rhythmically in place, moving their arms in strange gyrations, wildly intoxicated and dangerous. Swanson picked the closest. He guessed the distance at over six hundred feet, very close to the crossbow's maximum range. The quarrel head would not hit with enough impact to kill, so he slipped a bodkin, stiletto-like, long and slender, razor-honed steel that could sever a spinal cord or cut through four or five inches of muscle and bone, into the firing groove. It was a chance shot and it might give him away, but he needed time.

Swanson aimed a good half inch above the head of the Indian, hoping to catch him through a lung, but the shot was low, taking the brave in the stomach. The man began to flip and writhe on the ground. He would die, but it would be a long, painful death. Swanson took no pleasure in the thought. He kicked the mule into a trot.

Sun, ants and flies had been at the Mexican's head for three days and it no longer looked human. The fetid stench of both the man and the woman made him sick. The dog would not come close, but the mule was not bothered. To keep from vomiting, Swanson tossed loose dirt on the dead man's head until it was almost covered; then he tied the dead woman to a travois lashed to the saddle and headed at a trot for the canyon.

It took him half an hour to rope the corpse on to the mule. When he finished, he tied a blanket, cape-like, around the dead woman's neck and down her back to hide the two sticks of manzanita he had used to prop her upright. She looked grotesque, stiff and bloated, yet oddly militant and alive in her death pose. The effect was exactly what Swanson was aiming for. Strangely, for so warlike a people, the Apaches had a horror of death, and an equal horror of evil spirits. And in death this naked woman, with one breast cut off, the other savagely shredded, her abdomen split from breastbone to where her pubic area had once been, her eyes burned-out holes, looked frighteningly evil.

Once started, the mule would follow the trail to the bottom. Swanson slapped the animal hard on the rump and quickly, shouldering a heavy deerskin pack, moved out in an awkward, limping dogtrot. The pain in his leg was worse, and the wound had begun to bleed again. He stopped midway down the mountain and looked for the mule. It was moving in a careful gait, the dead woman rocking awkwardly on its back, what was left of her red hair blowing in a light breeze.

Swanson crouched in the chaparral until he heard the first frightened yell. The mule was standing at the foot of the slope with the woman still on its back, and panic-stricken Apaches were running away in fear.

He hit the open stretch of rocks between him and the wagons on a dead run, paying no mind to the fire in his thigh. He was past the nearest Apache before the man knew he was there. He ran on, twisting, waiting for the arrow from the warrior's bow. It never came. Up the slope he went, his legs driving, charging for the gap between the wagons. 'White man . . . amigo coming in . . . don't shoot,' he yelled. It did no good. The Hawken boomed out at him. But whoever was handling the weapon was a lousy shot and missed, and he was safe behind the wagons. He sprawled on his belly, breathing hard, pistol drawn waiting for the rush.

'Get ready . . . Cuidado,' he hissed. 'They may try to rush us now.' Out of the side of one eye, he saw what appeared to be a blotch of shadow move; he turned his head and looked directly into her face. He was stunned. A Catholic nun, little and worn looking, was on her knees praying, her eyes fixed on the gap between the wagons, the Hawken rifle smoking in her hands. Quickly, he glanced around the small enclosure; there was no one else. Still stunned, he looked back out from the shadows of the wagon into the bright sunlight. The mule and the woman were in plain view not more than fifty yards away. He glanced at the nun and realized she was staring at the dead woman. She was rocking back and forth quietly in her anguish, her lips moving in silent prayer.

'You okay, ma'am?' Swanson asked, not turning to look at her. She didn't answer. 'Ma'am,' he said, 'you need to get yourself ready. We're getting out of here in a few minutes.' The nun was deep in prayer and did not answer.

The ruse with the mule had worked better than he had hoped. The Apaches were falling back in panic into the hills. He decided to wait a few more minutes, then take the woman and slip out the north side and head into the high mountains. But it wasn't to be. The biggest Indian Swanson had ever seen put a stop to the confusion below. He was wearing a blue bandana tied the way slave women did up their hair, a leather vest with silver studs that had probably belonged to one of his Mexican victims, a breech-cloth and white pants tucked into deerskin boots. He stood a good foot taller than the braves milling nervously behind him. Even as a hundred yards, Swanson could almost feel the man's rage, like it was a physical thing.

He strode down out of the hills and yanked viciously at the mule's bridle until the animal reared. But the woman didn't dislodge and the Indian tore the blanket off the corpse, exposing the manzanita poles that propped her up. He pulled a knife, cut the poles, and then savagely shoved the body out of the saddle. Swanson heard the nun cry out in a gentle, hurt way. The Indian was kicking the corpse now, and the nun was praying out loud. Swanson cocked the crossbow quickly and inserted a quarrel, aiming under the wagon.

'No,' the woman said. Somehow the word was not a request, not an order, it was just a statement of what Swanson was going to do. Surprised, he glanced at her. She was still kneeling but now she was looking directly at him. He could tell from the paleness of her wrinkled face that she had spent her life inside a church. The clean neatness of her habit gave her thin, fine features a strange look of calm authority. Her eyes locked on his face with a steady gaze. She looked amazingly crisp and fresh, white against black, amid the dull, hot browns of the desert.

Uncomfortable, Swanson turned back to the Indians. The leader had disappeared, leaving his warriors to kick and slash at the dead woman's body, their confidence restored. 'Damn,' he whispered. Killing the big Apache might have sent the rest of them running. He picked a brave at random and dropped him with a head shot, the others scurried for cover.

Swanson heard the woman suck in her breath when he fired, and now she was praying out loud again. At one place in the prayer he heard her asking forgiveness for him. The thought made him feel awkward.

Neither of them spoke for a long time; the nun watching him and Swanson watching the rocks and hills. He felt her eyes on him. 'Lady, we aren't getting out of here without killing some of them.'

'God didn't send you to kill.' Her voice sounded firm but not angry.

'Ma'am, God didn't send me. I just came.' He squinted his eyes against the bright sunlight and scanned the canyon. 'And if we don't kill some, they're going to kill us. Anyhow,' he said, confused, 'you tried to kill me.'

'He sent you.' Her tone was matter-of-fact. 'And I only shot into the air.'

That at least explained why none of the shots from the Hawken had done any damage. The nun had been plugging the sky. As for God sending him, Swanson chose not to reply. Let her believe what she would.

'Do you have water?'

'In the canteens. But go light, we're going to be running hard in a few minutes.'

'The others can't run,' she said.

The words seemed to crash down on him. He rolled on his side and looked at the woman as she opened the pack and pulled out one of the canteens. 'Others?'

She stood without answering and hurried towards the cliff and a large rock. Kneeling, she disappeared into the side of the mountain. Quickly he loaded the Hawken and crawled back to the wagons. There were no Indians in sight, so he aimed at the rocks closest to the wagon and pulled the trigger. The big .54 calibre shell sent rock fragments flying. Figuring that would hold them for a while, he crawled around the rock. There was an opening in the mountain about as wide as a whisky barrel. He had seen these holes before. Twenty years earlier, prospectors had followed the road builders as they cut into the hills, searching for promising colour. When they found some, they would follow it a few feet or yards into the side of the

24

mountain. He looked in but couldn't see anything in the shadows.

'Who's in there?'

After he had waited a few seconds and gotten no answer, he drew his pistol and crawled in. The passage was cut out of sandstone and it was tight for his wide shoulders. He got stuck a couple of times, but after a few yards of crawling the passage widened some and he began to hear voices whispering ahead. Then he was in a larger vault-like cavern, fifteen by fifteen feet wide, and tall enough to stand in. A candle burned on top of a rock near the back, and he could see a black silhouette of a cross dancing against the walls; as his eyes adjusted, he began to see shapes in the room. It was refreshingly cool in the darkness.

'Who's in here?' he asked again.

'I and Sisters Elizabeth and Martha, and the children,' the nun said from somewhere in the blackness.

'Children? How many?'

'Seven.'

Swanson sat without saying anything for a few minutes, feeling suddenly very tired, and listened to the grateful sounds of the children drinking in the dark. It was obvious from the small animal-like noises they made that they had been dying of thirst.

'Seven,' he said.

'Seven,' the nun repeated.

He turned and crawled back to the wagons to sort things out in his head. After the cool darkness of the cavern, the air outside felt like a furnace. He sat down against the wall of the cliff, the rocks hot through his shirt, and began to reload the Hawken. The metal of the weapon burned when he touched it. Sweat began to run into his eyes and he tied his bandana around his forehead in the Apache way.

He had come down here to save the woman, he thought, nothing more. And now he had three women and seven children to worry about. Even if he could get all ten of them out without the Apaches knowing, which he doubted, there was no way he could hide that many people, especially kids, in the hills. With just the woman and following the hard rocks, moving back through the Apaches at night instead of running from them, he might have been able to escape. But not with seven kids, crying and making noise, falling behind.

He laid the loaded Hawken down next to him and pulled his pistol. He ran an oiled rag over the weapon, his eyes scanning the space under the wagons as he worked. The Apaches were not likely to charge an armed man in the light of day, but Swanson was not one to be caught off-guard. His head was throbbing. He guessed it was the change in temperature from the cave to the outside, or the wound in his leg, which was beginning to hurt badly again. He let his mind work over the facts a while. Every way he figured it, it came out the same: he was not getting out of here with ten people. For the first time in his life Nat Swanson felt trapped. He could run, but . . .

What had seemed like a fool's errand before now seemed like a desperate gamble gone terribly wrong; he could almost hear his mother's voice warning him against leaning too hard on a broken reed. He ran his hands through his hair, listening for the sound of her in his memory. There was nothing but the wind. She remained, as always, a shadowy presence in his thoughts. Still, there were things he half-remembered, and he felt she would have done the same thing he had; she, too, would have come for the old nun. He felt a little better. But not much.

Swanson heard a noise to his right and whirled, bringing the pistol up cocked and levelled at the old woman's head. She stared at him for a second and then walked over and returned the canteen to his pack.

'That's what guns do,' she said, the words hanging in the hot air.

When she didn't continue, Swanson asked, 'What?'

'They make you afraid.' She stood and walked over to him.

Ignoring the remark, he looked up at her and said, 'You shouldn't stand; you'll be killed.'

'Perhaps,' she answered, kneeling down beside him, a candle and a small leather purse in her hands, 'but only if the Lord wants me to die. And I won't die afraid.' She smiled at him. 'Now let me see your leg.'

'It's fine. It's just a hole.'

'Let me see your leg, please,' she said firmly, lighting the candle with a match and sticking it in the sand. 'From the amount of blood on your pants, it's more than just a hole, and the children need you.'

Swanson looked into the woman's face for a few seconds and realized she wasn't going to let him alone; he stretched his leg out so she could see it. The wound was oozing badly. She opened the purse and took out a small knife and heated the blade in the flame of the candle. Swanson watched her thin, delicate hands as she worked. They were old hands, mottled with liver spots but steady, and it was obvious she had dressed wounds before. She was wearing a wedding ring and this surprised him. Laying

27

the small knife down, she took a pair of scissors and cut the buckskin leggings so she could get at the wound. It wasn't pretty. The entry hole was small enough, but the bullet had hit bone and flattened out and the wound was deep and ugly and seeping clear fluid and blood, and it was dirty. The skin around it was a festering purple colour. The woman began to reheat the blade of the knife.

'What is your plan?' she asked.

Swanson sat staring blindly at the bullet hole for a few seconds. 'I don't know.'

She seemed a little startled and then went back to heating the knife. He was thinking that if he'd known about the other nuns and the kids he might not have come at all, but he didn't say it out loud.

She was watching him closely again. 'You would have,' she said after a few moments.

Swanson jumped. 'Would have what?'

'You were thinking you wouldn't have helped if you'd known there were so many of us.' She waited a second, still staring into his face. 'You still would have.' Her voice was matter-of-fact.

He looked into her eyes, surprised she had guessed his thoughts. Then he shrugged it off. He had never not had a choice in his entire life, even if the choice had been to die. He still had choices. He pulled his eyes away from hers and shook his head, looking out at the brilliant sunlight and the canyon. Sweat was running down his neck.

'This will hurt. Before I start, I want to thank you for saving the children. They were dying.'

'How long had they been without water?'

'Two days. But it wasn't only the water. It was the fear.'

28

Swanson didn't understand. He waited for her to explain, but she was bending over the wound. 'So what's changed?'

'They know God sent you to save them.' She smiled at him.

The words seemed to slap at his face. She began to run the knife hard around the edge of the wound, leaving a thin trail of blood welting behind the sharp blade.

'Listen, lady –' Swanson started to say, before the pain slammed him upside of his head and he went unconscious.

It was late evening when Swanson awoke. The hurt in his leg was awful. His vision was fuzzy and he couldn't focus on the white bandage made from a woman's undergarment, but he didn't need to see it to know the leg beneath the wrapping hurt as if she'd driven a wooden stake into his thigh. When his eyes finally focused, he saw a younger nun with a pudgy, cherub-like face kneeling in front of him looking concerned. She was maybe twenty. She smiled a gentle smile that filled something up inside him.

'I'm Sister Martha. Would you like some water?' He didn't want any. She turned her head and called softly, 'Sister St Agnes, he's awake.'

The old nun came and stood over him. 'Good. God would have never forgiven me if you'd died.' Her eyes were laughing good-naturedly.

'What did you do to my leg?' He was fighting back a moan struggling out of the depth of him.

'It was dirty. I cut the flesh away and opened it up inside and took the bullet out.' She was walking back towards a small campfire of burning mesquite in the centre of the enclosed ground. 'It will heal now.'

29

It took Swanson a few minutes to regain his bearings and to remember where he was. The younger nun continued to watch him until he returned her stare, then she averted her eyes shyly. His thoughts were on the old nun; this woman who moaned and prayed over the deaths of savages – savages who were out to kill them – but who cut his leg to pieces as casually as if she were cleaning chickens. She didn't figure so easy. He watched the flickering light from the campfire for a few minutes, thinking about her, before he realized what was bothering him. He jumped.

'Lady, put that out!' he yelled, rolling toward the fire.

The two nuns caught him gently by the shoulders. He felt weak. 'Don't,' the old one said, 'you'll hurt yourself and you'll scare the children.'

'Scare the children, hell.' His voice was rising. 'You're going to get yourself and them killed with that fire.'

'I insist you do not swear in front of the children,' she said, turning back to the fire. 'They have to eat. As soon as the meal is finished, I'll put the fire out. Thank you for your concern.'

Swanson was holding himself up with one arm, staring at the back of the woman's black robes as she worked over the campfire. He couldn't believe her, she was crazy. He realized that the younger nun, Sister Martha, was still supporting his shoulder. As he started to pull away, pain tore through his leg and he caught himself.

'Are you all right?' the young nun asked.

'I'm okay,' he mumbled, crawling back to the wagons. He picked up the Hawken and scanned the darkening shadows of the canyon. His leg was driving him crazy with pain but he forced himself to think about the Apaches. He couldn't see anything out of the ordinary, but he knew that meant nothing. The Mimbres were desert mountain people. They could lie in ambush a yard from a man in barren sand and not be discovered until it was too late. The only chance he had of spotting one was to study the road and the canyon until he had committed every bush, every rock, every patch of colour to memory, and then to wait for some small change. His thoughts were distracted by the sounds of cooking.

'Hurry up, lady,' he hissed.

'In God's own time,' she responded.

Swanson heard soft scuffling noises behind him and he turned his head to see the last of the children crawl out of the hole in the mountain. It was almost completely dark now and they were small darker shapes squatting forlornly against the mountainside. There was a larger shadow at the end of the line. Swanson watched it suspiciously for a few seconds until he realized it was the third nun.

'Ahhh, Sister Elizabeth, children, there you are,' the old nun said. 'Isn't it wonderful to be out in the night air.' Her voice was as light and breezy as if they were on a summer picnic. 'Children, I'd like you to meet the man who has come to take you out of here.'

Swanson shot her an angry glance, but she wasn't looking at him.

'I'm sorry,' she said loudly, leaning over a large pot, 'but I'm afraid I don't know your name, sir.'

Swanson waited a few seconds and then said, 'Nat Swanson.' He turned his head towards the night and the canyon sounds.

'Nat Swanson,' she said gaily. 'What a strong-sounding name. Children, come for your dinner and say hello to Mr Swanson. Jessica, you first.'

'Hello, Mr Swanson,' the small voice said.

Swanson watched the darkness for a few seconds longer, but the innocence of the voice tugged at him and he turned, instantly bothered by what he saw. Jessica was small, maybe nine, thin and dirty looking in a rag dress; her tiny face seemed far too old.

'Hello, Jessica,' he said, glancing at the nun. She was smiling approvingly.

There were twins, Betty and Nan, perhaps ten or eleven, but it was difficult to be certain because of their starved condition. Next came a gangly girl of about thirteen wearing a filthy calico dress and swollen with child.

'Tell Mr Swanson your name, child,' the older nun said softly. The girl didn't speak. She stood holding her stomach awkwardly as if she wanted to set it down and watched the flames of the fire. 'Well, that's okay,' the nun said pleasantly. 'Mr Swanson, we don't know this lovely child's name yet, but we have christened her Millie until we do.'

Then two little girls, Bonnie and Anna, six or seven years old, came into the light of the campfire. They were holding hands as if they were lost and they were as dirty and poorly clothed as the others. The last child would not leave the shadows until the third nun brought him forward.

'And this, Mr Swanson,' the old nun said proudly, 'is the man of our party, Matthew.'

The boy was in the worst shape of all of them. He was perhaps eight. His face had been disfigured by fire. Swanson had seen those kinds of scars before. They had been done on purpose. He was almost naked, and he limped badly on a leg that had been broken and not set.

'Nice to meet you, Matthew.' The boy stared at the ground. He looked ashamed to speak. The third nun was holding him gently by the shoulders. Swanson glanced at her. She was tall and thin, in her thirties, and had a very pleasant face. He remembered her name was Sister Elizabeth. She was proper, proud and pretty, and he watched her for longer than he felt comfortable. She was a handsome woman. She was staring at the top of the little boy's head.

After the last child had been served, the old nun put dirt on the fire and seemingly total darkness fell on the party. Swanson sat by the wagons, listening to the night, amazed the Indians had not fired on the campfire light. It was still and hot. Somewhere off in the distance a hunting owl sounded, once, then twice more. He focused on the sound and decided it was the real thing, not an Indian imitator. Sister Martha brought him a plate of beans and half a cup of water. He ate, thinking about the children and the old nun. Then, with his plate half full and without realizing it, he fell asleep.

The cave had the faint odour of burned incense and a snug feel about it. The three nuns and seven children fitted nicely into it, and there was a clean starkness that reminded the three sisters of a monastery, and this gave them great comfort. The children were asleep in a long row on the soft, sandy floor. They lay peacefully on the blankets spread for them, and for the first night none were crying, none shaking. The heels of Sister Martha's plain black shoes thumped softly against the large rock she was sitting on. Her face was beaming and she was leaning forward with both of her hands on her knees, the heavy

33

cloth of her habit spread over the rock. Sister Elizabeth was kneeling nearby, rubbing a pan that had been used for supper with clean sand. A large candle burned on a smaller rock near the back wall of the cave casting a warm glow over the children's faces, softening the gauntness and sadness somewhat. In the deeper shadows sat Sister St Agnes, her thin back propped against the sandstone wall, her eyes closed.

Sister Martha looked lovingly over the faces of the children. 'Wasn't he wonderful to come?' she whispered. 'He's a sainted man to risk his life for theirs.'

Sister Elizabeth poured the sand from the pan and set it aside, reaching for a plate. 'I don't think we should enroll him among the saints.' Her voice was low and carrying a practical edge to it. 'We don't know why he came.' She scrubbed hard at the plate.

'He came to save the children,' Sister Martha said. Her words were gentle, but slightly worried sounding.

'Perhaps, but perhaps not.'

Sister Martha was sitting up straight now, her hands clasped together in her lap as if they ached. 'I don't understand,' she whispered louder. 'Why else would he come?'

'I don't know why. I just suspect he's not a saint,' Sister Elizabeth insisted. 'Sister says he killed one man. And I don't believe in my heart he'll stay and save the children. God wouldn't send a man like that.' She worked over the plate longer than it took to clean it.

Neither woman spoke after that. Sister Martha did not know what to say, and Sister Elizabeth felt she had said too much and was sorry for it.

'He was sent to save the children,' Sister St Agnes said

from the shadows, her voice gentle but firm. 'We must not question God's gifts.'

Out of respect, Sister Elizabeth did not say anything else, but in her heart she did not believe that Sister St Agnes was correct.

A full hunter's moon had crested the far mountain, splashing the canyon with a gentle light, by the time Swanson awoke. He moved his hand down slowly until he felt the comforting chill of the revolver's handle. His leg felt somewhat better. He lay peering out at the grey shapes of the rocks, probing the familiar sounds of the night. A second later, he realized someone was sitting near him and he tensed.

'The moon's beautiful tonight,' the old nun said softly.

His leg began to throb and he pulled himself slowly into a sitting position and studied the wagons and the shadows on the road. He watched her from the side of his eye.

'Tell me about the children,' he said.

'There's not much to tell, Mr Swanson.' She was looking up at the stars overhead. 'We learned six months ago a Mexican town had ransomed ten American children from a band of Comanche Indians in Sonora and wanted more money than they had paid for their release or they would sell them as slaves. Unfortunately, no one could come up with the names of their next of kin or the money, so our church raised it and Sisters Martha, Ruth and Elizabeth and I came for them.'

'Where are the other three?'

'They died before we could get to them,' she said quietly.

He didn't speak for a while, thinking about the children

35

huddled in the dark of the cave. Then he thought of the sisters, Martha and Elizabeth, and felt better. 'I'm sorry they died.'

'I'm certain heaven is a wonderful place to grow up in, Mr Swanson.'

He looked at her profile in the dark. 'Do you believe all that stuff you say, ma'am?'

'Do you?'

He should have known she wouldn't defend herself. That wasn't her way. He sat thinking for a while and then he said, 'Yes.'

'Good, so do I.'

Swanson thought about her answer for a long time. Later, after the moon had risen to full height, he spoke again. 'Why won't the boy talk?'

He felt her shift on the sand beside him. She waited a few seconds as she resettled her cloak before answering. 'He can't very well. The Mexicans who bought him told us the Indians had cut his tongue out because he wouldn't stop crying for his parents. And now I guess he's ashamed or afraid to try.'

Swanson heard a rock fall somewhere out in the darkness. And, a little later, another. They were small sounds, but neither was a natural occurrence. He twisted his body slightly and slipped the pistol out of the holster. The nun was sitting on the other side of him, a few feet away, and he was certain she hadn't noticed. He turned his head slowly, back and forth, to pick up any sounds in the hot air, and he moved his eyes away from the direction of the noise, looking that way from the side so he could see better.

'It's near the wagon,' the nun said softly. 'Mr Swanson, don't shoot.'

'Shhh,' he whispered. He could see it now. A piece of shadow had seemed to grow from nothing at the far end of the wagon. It didn't move for a long time, then he realized it was closer, and moving closer still. He raised the pistol. As he was aiming down the revolver's long barrel, he felt her hand on his arm.

'Don't,' she said.

He hesitated and then he saw the shadow rise and trot into the open. The dog sat a few yards away from them, staring out in the direction of Santa Fe, staring as if he could see all the way there. He looked rested and fit, and while Swanson was glad to see him, he was angry about the scare.

'Ma'am, tell the children not to touch that animal, he'll tear an arm off. He flat can't be trusted.' The dog continued to peer out into the dark distance, ignoring them both.

'What's its name?'

'I don't know,' he said.

'What do you call it?'

'Dog.'

'Well then, I guess that's its name.'

Swanson and the old nun sat together in silence for a while longer. With the dog in the enclosure, he felt less tense and he spread his saddle blanket and lay back on the sand. He watched the stars for a time and then said, 'What's your name, ma'am?'

'Sister St Agnes,' her voice sounding as if she had been far away in her thoughts.

'How do you get to be a saint?'

'I'm not one.' She chuckled. 'That's the name I took at the convent.'

37

She had a young laugh, and it seemed odd in a woman of her years. In fact, much about her and what had happened to him over the past twenty-four hours seemed odd. He couldn't figure it. She didn't scare easy, he'd give her that much.

'There were two Saint Agneses,' she said, absently.

'Two?'

'Yes. One very famous. Agnes of Montepulciano. She was born in Tuscany in 1268 AD.'

'I've never heard of Tuscany.'

'It's in Italy. Anyway, I'm not named after her. She established a nunnery in Montepulciano and had a lot of visions. And a great many miracles and other remarkable occurrences are attributed to her.'

'But you're not named after her.'

'No. She was too grand a saint for me to be named after.' She smiled. 'I'm named after the little Saint Agnes.'

'What did she do?'

'She was martyred in Rome in 304 AD at the age of thirteen.'

'Why?'

'She refused to marry and instead she consecrated her maidenhood to God. And when the Roman persecution of the Christians began, she offered herself in martyrdom. She was executed by being stabbed in the throat by a centurion's sword.'

'At thirteen, because she wouldn't marry?'

'No. At thirteen because she wouldn't deny God.'

'Why did you take her name?'

'I guess I identified with her. I was seventeen when I entered the convent. And when my father, who didn't like the idea, told me that someday I would want to marry and have children, I told him that I had already married God.'

'He didn't like that?'

'He didn't like that at all,' she said. 'And your name? Where does it come from?'

Swanson continued to look at the stars without saying anything. Then he sat up and shrugged his shoulders.

'From my parents.'

She said, 'Well, I guessed that much. Were you named after your father . . . your grandfather?'

'My dad's name was John. I had a grandfather name of Richard.'

Sister St Agnes watched his face for a few minutes and then leaned back on her hands and looked up at the sky and the black silhouettes of the canyon walls.

'It's a lovely night.'

They didn't talk for a long time then. When Swanson finally spoke he was running a strip of fresh rawhide through the holster of his pistol.

'Your church in New Mexico or Texas?'

'Pennsylvania.'

Swanson turned his head and looked at the dark, thin shape of the old nun sitting beside him. 'That's a piece. How did you get here?'

'By train, stagecoach, wagon, horse and foot.'

Swanson stared at the holster for a long while, then said, 'Why would you come all the way down here to a place like this, a place you don't know?'

She didn't answer right away. Finally, she said, 'Faith.' She looked at the side of his face. 'Does that make any sense to you?'

'Not much.'

'We came because of Jesus Christ, Mr Swanson. The children were suffering and alone. We came to give them God's love.'

'No matter what the price?'

'I don't understand.'

'Even if it costs you and the sisters your lives?'

She smiled. 'You make us sound so important. We are only three small instruments in God's hand.' She was smiling broadly now, her two large front teeth plainly visible. 'You don't smile enough, Mr Swanson. God loves a cheerful giver.'

'You aren't from these parts,' he said quickly. 'You don't know the Apache.'

'They're God's children, same as you or I.'

'And the lady, the Mexican, the boy and the others?' He was still watching her.

'Ignorance and evil.' She stood up as if the conversation had suddenly pushed her away, dusted her robes and then moved from him toward the far side of the enclosure.

'Where did the Mexicans go who were driving your wagons?' he called softly after her.

She stopped and looked back at him. 'They ran off the first night.'

'Do you think they made it?'

He watched her. She was smaller than he had first thought but she stood straight and proud, her frail shoulders squared against the massive canyons. He was surprised he had asked her the question. There was no way she could answer it. He knew that.

'I've prayed for it.' She turned away again.

'How often do your prayers work?'

She turned quickly, looking down at him, the first hint

of annoyance flickering at the wrinkled corner of her mouth. Then she smiled. 'They brought me you,' she said, turning and walking to where the dog sat. The animal got up and moved away a few yards and then lay down and watched her.

He couldn't see her very well in the dark, but he knew she was praying. He heard his name once and the awkward feeling came over him again. He figured the chances of the two Mexicans couldn't have been good. The Apaches would have expected just such a move and would have been waiting. Nevertheless, there was a chance one of the two might have got through, and if he knew anything about staying alive in the desert, he could make it to Sonora in seven or eight days. Swanson didn't hang on the chance, but he tucked it away in his head as a possible way out. There weren't many.

Sister St Agnes sat studying the dark silhouette of the man sitting a few yards away. He was one of God's mysteries. He was plainly handsome enough to be an angel of God, she thought, perhaps the most handsome man she had ever seen in her life. But his looks seemed the only thing even partly angelic about him. She had seen enough wounds to know that the thin scar that ran the length of his jaw had been made by a knife, and the hole in his leg had been made by a bullet. And he had already killed one man in front of her and was ready to kill more. And he had used poor Sister Ruth's torn body as a decoy, debasing it as much as the savages had. He swore a great deal. He showed no sign of religious feelings.

She couldn't answer the questions pounding in her head. She tipped her chin forward on to her breast. 'Dear

God,' she whispered, 'I have never questioned Your wisdom or Your authority ... I'm not questioning them now. I only wonder ... wonder why You sent this man to save the children. And how I should deal with him. I thank You for Your blessings and Your guidance.' She stared at her hands, knowing that she had received no answers.

Day Two...

_____

The horned toad had wiggled itself down into the sand leaving only the spikes on its back and the longer horns on its blunt-snouted head exposed. He guessed it was hunting flies. Swanson was leaning against a large rock in the shade watching the lizard hunt. The Hawken lay across his lap. It was close to noon and Sisters Elizabeth and Martha had just finished feeding the children their dinner. Sister St Agnes was in the cave, probably praying, he figured. The dog was sleeping on its back in the shade of the wagon, its long legs helter-skelter in the air. The lizard dropped what seemed like a clear shade over its eye, then it disappeared. Lying half buried in the sand, it looked like a newspaper drawing he had once seen of something called a dinosaur.

The heat was brutal.

Swanson scanned the road and then looked to his right at the children. They were sitting quietly in a band of shade next to the cliff. They were tired and listless and hot. Their faces were burned and he knew that their throats were as parched as his own. He searched the sand around him and began to pick up and examine small pebbles. Some he kept. Some he tossed away. Then with a movement so quick it was hard to see, he grabbed the squat little lizard out of the sand.

The twins were closest to him. 'Come take a look.' He had pulled his sombrero off and laid it over the hand holding the horned toad.

The girls stood slowly and helped the little ones, Bonnie and Anna, to their feet. Jessica came too. Only Millie and the boy, Matthew, stayed where they were. The five girls formed a half circle around him.

'What you got?' Anna asked.

Sister Elizabeth had wandered over and was standing looking out at the canyon, listening. He knew she didn't approve of him.

'I've got a Texas devil under my hat,' he said.

'Go on!'

'I do.'

'Naw,' said Jessica, 'there ain't no such thing as a Texas devil.'

'There must be because I caught him. He's under my hat. Go ahead and take a peek.'

Jessica reached a hand out slowly towards his sombrero and then jerked it back and ran in place on the tips of her toes for a few seconds. The others shrieked with the thrill of it.

'If you've got him, what's he look like?'

'Well, he's got horns on his head . . . and spikes on his tail and when he gets mad he spits blood.'

The children screamed and laughed.

Sister Elizabeth had turned and she was staring angrily at him, her arms akimbo. He paid her no mind.

'I've got him sure enough. But before I show him to you, I want you each to take a pebble out of my hand and put it under your tongue and keep it there.'

46

'Why?' It was Anna. She was small and lightly built, but she was smart and bright-eyed.

'Because it will make you feel better. These are magic pebbles.'

He held his hand flat and let each select a pebble. They put them in their mouths.

'Good. Now let me count to five . . . one, two, three, four . . . and five. There, Feel better?'

They all nodded. He knew they would. The small stones would help them fight the thirst by drawing saliva into their mouths which they could swallow.

'Good. Now who wants to be the first to see the Texas devil?'

'I will.' It was Betty, the eleven-year-old. She looked scared but she reached a hand and grabbed the crown of the sombrero and yanked it off. As she did, Swanson shoved the lizard at her and growled. She jumped up and backward and the other children yelled and ran for the pure joy of it.

'Really, Mr Swanson. You should be ashamed of yourself scaring the children and telling them you have the devil in your hand. What kind of nonsense do you want to put in their heads?'

Swanson stroked the lizard's belly gently with his finger. He didn't look up at Sister Elizabeth. 'I was just trying to give them some fun. They don't look like they've had much lately.'

They came back giggling and ready to run.

'Let us see him.'

Swanson held the horned toad out for them and one by one they touched his spiny backside. Sister Elizabeth was walking toward the cave.

'You said he could spit blood.'

Swanson glanced across the enclosure to make sure the nun wasn't watching him. 'And he can. Stand back.'

When they had cleared a pathway in front of him, Swanson teased the lizard with his finger for a moment, then pointed its head toward the open area and squeezed his stomach some. It wasn't enough to hurt him, but the pressure made him nervous that he was about to be eaten and the little dinosaur let go. A bright red stream of blood spurted out of one of his eyes a full five feet across the sand. The children's eyes got wide. Anna stooped and touched her finger to the red trail on the sand.

'It's really blood!' she screamed. 'He is the Texas devil!'

The children ran away again.

A few minutes later, Jessica came back and asked for the Texas devil. Swanson gave it to her with the promise she wouldn't pester it. She took the little creature to the other children and they spent an hour or so playing with it and laughing. He felt better.

Later, when it was close to evening and the strip of shadow near the rocks had reached halfway across the enclosure, when the Gambel's quail had started calling each other for the night roost, Anna came and stood in front of Swanson, holding something behind her back. Her face was thin and smudged with dirt. She looked happy.

'I have something for you, Mr Swanson.'

'That's nice. What, diamonds?'

'No. It's flowers.' She held them out to him. They were three small desert lilacs. 'They're to thank you with.'

'Well, Anna, they're very nice but you didn't have to thank me. I had as much fun with the Texas devil as you.'

'But that's not why I'm thanking you.'

'No? Why then?'

She seemed surprised. ''Cause you came to save us, silly. I thanked God just the way Sister St Agnes said, but I should thank you, too. My momma always told me that.'

Swanson nodded. 'You must miss your mother a lot.'

'Yeah, but you're going to take me home.' She gazed at his face. He didn't look up at her.

'You are, aren't you?'

'Sure I am.'

Swanson sat staring at the flowers in his hand as the little girl walked back to the others. *You are, aren't you?* The words seemed to pound like a small fist in his head. He had no idea how he could get seven kids and three women out of this sandstone hole in the ground. And even if he could, the Apaches would be after them an hour after they left the enclosure.

Later, after Sisters Elizabeth and Martha had put the children to bed in the cave, after the moon had jumped the rim of the canyon, Swanson walked over to where the old nun sat holding her Bible and staring off into the darkness of the canyon beyond the wagons. She looked up at him and smiled. 'Hello, Mr Swanson. May I help you?'

'It's about the children.'

'Yes?'

'It's about what you've been telling them about me.'

'What's that?'

'About me being sent here from God . . .'

'Yes?'

He cleared his throat. 'It just isn't so – that's all. And it isn't good to fill their heads with that kind of a promise.'

'What promise?'

'That I'm going to get them out of here.' He stopped talking and looked out at the night for a while. 'I can't keep it.'

The old nun continued to stare up at him. The smile had left her face and her lips were pressed together. Then she looked down at the Bible in her hands. 'Mr Swanson, it may be hard for you to believe – and I certainly don't blame you for feeling the way you do – but you were sent here from God to save the children. And, with God's help, you'll do it.'

Swanson stared at her for a long time and then said, 'God better be ready to do a heap of helping.'

Day Three...

They ran low on water around noon. The Apaches did two things to make it worse. The first was not the most troubling. Sometime during the night, they had crawled up on to the road and hung a deer intestine filled with water on a stick, and started it dripping. Try as he might, Swanson couldn't keep his eyes off it. And when he caught himself calculating the distance between the bag and the wagons, he raised the barrel of the Hawken and blew it away. The Apaches jeered at him and yelled taunts from the safety of the rocks, but they were surprised. Most thirsty men didn't destroy water, even if it was driving them mad. In their collective, superstitious mind, the Apaches began to think at that moment that perhaps the white man they had cornered was not mortal. They had still not recovered from their fright over the dead black robe.

He didn't know how to deal with the second. They had done this during the night as well. Some fifty yards off, down the rocky slope in front of them and halfway up the sandy rise of the stream bed, sat the putrifying body of the dead woman staring blindly at them. They had sharpened both ends of a thick mesquite branch, driving one end into the soft sand and the other up the woman's rectum, impaling her in a sitting position. The body's intestines had begun to bloat and were sticking out of the open abdomen, the heat turning the corpse a purplish green. Only the old nun would look at it directly and Swanson had noticed her watching the body more than once, her lips moving in silent prayer.

That evening they made the children sit facing the wall of rock as they ate their supper. Midway through the meal, an Apache, hidden behind boulders a few yards to the left of the corpse, began to use the body as a target for his arrows. He shouted obscenities in broken English each time an arrow struck. Swanson watched two arrows penetrate the woman's head. The old nun said a prayer he could hear and went back to talking loudly and gaily with the children. But he had seen the little boy's hands trembling, and a few seconds later another child dropped her water cup in the sand. They were whimpering softly now and Sister Elizabeth was holding the boy in her lap and stroking his hair. Swanson looked away from them and back out to the large rock where the Apache lay concealed. Something bad was rising in his throat. He had felt it before many times and he knew he couldn't stop it.

Suddenly it tore lose, and he ordered the women and the children into the cave. The younger ones were badly frightened by the tone in his voice and most of them were crying as they left. The old woman watched him, but said nothing until he grabbed the Hawken rifle and crawled under the wagon.

'They don't know any better.' Her voice was sharp.

'They're about to learn,' he snapped. He waved the dog out of the enclosure toward the dead woman. It went

54

down the hill in long bounds, tumbling in an awkward twist of legs and dust at the river bottom, then started for the rocks where the hidden Indian had been taunting Swanson and shooting arrows at the dead woman. Swanson pulled the heavy butt of the Hawken in tight against his shoulder, and as the dog darted behind the rocks he sighted on the biggest. Behind him the old nun kept repeating, 'Hail Mary, full of Grace . . .' There was a frightened yell, then a louder shout, and suddenly an Apache stumbled away from the rocks below, the dog tearing at his hands. Swanson brought the notch into the centre of the man's head and pulled the trigger. The big gun boomed and the Indian's skull exploded. He picked up the crossbow and waited for the dog to flush the next one.

He wounded another this way as the old nun prayed louder, then decided the dog was at too great a risk and whistled it back to the wagons. The old nun would not look at him or talk to him.

The children came out later and finished eating their meagre meal in silence and drank the last of the water. They didn't look at him, except for the boy. The three nuns sat with their backs to the rocks, not eating or drinking, but carrying on a lively conversation among themselves and the children. A conversation as fine and light and gay as any Swanson had ever heard at a sewing bee or social throughout the territory. They talked about all the wonderful clothes the children were going to have, the dolls, the hoops and sticks, the puppets and other delights awaiting them. They talked about baths filled with sudsy water, told them about Pennsylvania and how green it was, and the way the farms looked at harvest time, and about sledding and snow and how to make angels in it. They talked about towns and houses and schools and books. Swanson sat away from them, listening, deeper in the darkness near one of the wagons where he could watch the road and the rocks. His leg was hurting again.

There was enough moonlight so he could see them clearly. The old nun led the conversation. Her laughter seemed to ripple through the children's little bodies somehow and gave them new life. Sister Elizabeth was more solemn and reserved, but it was obvious as she told them about maple trees and syruping on winter nights that she loved the children. He saw her glance at him once and then look quickly away. Sister Martha was a Cochin hen, fat and energetic, moving hurriedly among the line of children to brush hair out of eyes, to pinch a cheek lovingly, to hug generously. The old nun was sitting between the two younger sisters and she didn't move; she sat spinning her magical stories, her bright eyes approving of all she surveyed.

The children had begun to talk and even laugh some, but not the pregnant girl or the boy, Matthew. They sat at opposite ends of the line, like small, brave sentries, watching the others but not permitting themselves to participate. The girl, Millie, was sitting with her thin legs stretched out before her and leaning back on her hands. The enormous bulge of her stomach lay on her as if it were a large rock that had pinned her awkwardly to the ground. She watched the nuns closely but stayed carefully at the outer edge of the conversation. The nuns fussed over her a moment, but she remained distant in her thoughts.

Swanson looked at the boy now. His small arms were folded across his thin chest and gave the appearance that he was holding himself. He was rocking back and forth where he sat, his eyes staring into the mountain as though he could see something inside it that was dear to him. The boy paid no attention to the conversation of the three nuns except at one point, when Sister Elizabeth said, 'Your Father in heaven loves you', he raised his eyes and stared into the nun's face searchingly. Something tightened in Swanson's throat and he forced himself to look away from the scarred face and back out at the shadows of the desert night. He thought about the life waiting for him in California.

This day had been the hottest yet, and the night air lay like a warm blanket over the land. The dog was sleeping under one of the wagons. A dry stirring of air came up the rock slope bringing with it the sickeningly sweet smell of the decaying corpse. As the heavy, fetid odour passed over them, the conversation behind him stopped for a moment, then Sister St Agnes started talking about an old pony that stole apples.

Swanson took a piece of poor jerky from his pack and walked over to the wagon where the animal lay. He squatted down and looked at it. It was stretched out, resting its head on its paws. It rolled its eyes so it could watch him without lifting its head.

'Good job.' He tossed the jerky out toward the dog's head. The animal whirled, still lying on the sand, the jerky now between its paws, its lips pulled back in a vicious snarl. Swanson fell backwards. 'You ungrateful son-of-a—'

'Mr Swanson,' Sister St Agnes interrupted in a bright

voice. She had seen the dog snarl. 'Dog seems a bit upset,' she said. She watched as the animal wolfed the jerky in one hungry gulp.

Swanson looked over his shoulder at it. His face was red. He jerked a thumb at it. 'He's always upset. He's a cantankerous, irritable, evil-tempered animal. I should have shot him long ago.'

'Why haven't you?'

Swanson looked at her, surprised, and, after a few seconds, he said, 'I guess because he's the best Indian dog in the territory.'

The sister was standing with her arms crossed over her chest. 'Well, that explains why you keep him . . . but what I can't understand is why he keeps you.'

'He doesn't like anyone . . . but I guess he likes me best of all.'

Later, when they had taken the children into the cave to sleep, when the bats were stitching through the night sky, the old nun came again to talk. This time, she came slowly as though reluctant, standing beside him for a few minutes and staring out at the canyon.

'It's beautiful, isn't it?' she said quietly.

'Things have looked better to me.' He didn't raise his head.

She sat next to him. 'We're out of water and low on food, Mr Swanson,' she said softly.

'I know.'

'How long can the children last without it?' She was making busy with her hands, straightening her robes, her lips drawn into a thin, tight smile.

'Without water, if they stay in the cave, three, maybe four days.'

She sat without saying anything for a few minutes, and then she turned and looked at the side of his face and smiled warmly. 'That's a long time. Perhaps the Indians will get tired of waiting and they'll leave.'

To another woman, Swanson would have lied. To the old nun he said, 'No, they won't.'

'Then perhaps someone will come down the road,' she offered.

'The American Cavalry is about the only one foolish enough to use this road, and they avoid it.'

'Then maybe it will rain and the Indians will realize how futile it is to wait any longer,' she tried again.

Swanson stared hard at her face for a moment. She didn't quit. 'Ma'am, that isn't going to happen either. It rains so little around here that when it finally does, people think it's a wonderment.'

She didn't respond right away. When she did, her voice was still fresh sounding. 'Mr Swanson, I don't believe you understand how fortunate you are.'

'Fortunate? Stuck in a rock hole with three women, seven children, no water and no way out isn't fortunate, ma'am.' He was sorry as soon as he had said it.

'You were chosen by God to rescue these children.' She stared at her hands for a moment and then said, 'I don't understand why you were selected or why you persist in doing the things you do, but the fact remains, God chose you. That makes you one of the most fortunate people in the world. Few are chosen, Mr Swanson.' She stood abruptly and walked over to the cave. Swanson followed her with his eyes. She stopped at the entrance and looked back at him. 'You'll find a way.'

The canopy of night sky was punctured in a thousand

59

places with sparkling light, the air was hot and still, night birds sang somewhere higher up the canyon walls far above where Swanson sat shaking his head. 'I was not chosen,' he muttered.

The screams began hours later, and they were barely human. They were unholy. Swanson knew what they meant the moment he heard them. The Mexicans had not made it. The old nun scrambled out of the hole and hurried over to him. She stood listening for a few minutes, crossed herself and then walked quickly and sat down before the hole in the mountain, using her small back to block the sounds from entering the cave. She prayed until beads of sweat appeared on her forehead. An hour later, the screams stopped and she fell into an exhausted sleep.

Swanson sat looking at the deed. He couldn't see much in the moon's light but the lines and shapes of the letters were all he needed to see to visualize it. Later, he folded it and put it back in his vest pocket. It was the only permanent thing he had ever had. It was hard for him to understand the feeling. After the age of eight he had had no family, no home. All his life he had fought other people's battles and all he had ever owned was their hatred. Now, even though he didn't have so much as a single cow yet, he had a place were he belonged, he had something worthwhile to do, a line of work. He had begun to think of himself as a cattle rancher. The thought felt good.

He went back to staring at the old nun's face. He waited until he was certain she was sound asleep, then he began to pack his things. Finished, he checked the caplock on the Hawken and quietly leaned the rifle against the wall next to the woman. He studied her face for a few seconds more in the moonlight. In sleep she looked dead and he felt something bump inside his chest. He turned and shouldered his pack and started across the enclosure. He did not see the old nun open her eyes and watch him leave.

He waited in the rocks on the far side of the dry river bed for a long time, watching up the slope to the dark shapes of the wagons, waiting to see if they had spotted his leaving and would move against the women and children. He was surprised that he hadn't run in to any Apaches near the road and the wagons. He didn't believe they had all pulled out to help torture the Mexicans. The dog sat watching the hills behind them, off in the direction of the screams that had started again and were coming with unnerving regularity. The moon had passed over the canyon and cast the rocks and sand into a darkness that made it hard to see more than a few feet in any direction. Convinced that for whatever reason they had not seen him, he moved carefully up a small trail, the crossbow in his hands.

The wound in his leg began to hurt and bleed again. He kept moving. The trail was steep and bordered by ocotillo plants and yuccas, and with the moon down over the far canyon wall it was fairly dark. Somewhere higher in the hills he heard the squeal and then the grunts of a band of javelinas. He figured they were probably fighting over agave leaves or beavertail cactus. The thought of the wild pigs and the cactus pads made him remember his hunger. He kept moving, his eyes working the trail ahead of him. Suddenly, he stopped. He could see something shadowy and big in the rocks a few feet to his left. The dog was nowhere in sight. He cursed it under his breath as he went down to his knees. The sound of a voice jolted through his body. It was Apache. And there wasn't one, there were five or maybe six of them on both sides of the trail not more than a few feet from where he crouched.

They were eating and talking low. Blood began to pound in his temples as another dark shape came down the trail towards him. He had walked right into the middle of a pack of them. They hadn't noticed him yet and he stood up and turned slowly around and froze. Another was climbing towards him from the trail below, some five or six yards away. He was surrounded. He was close enough to smell cooked meat and hear chewing and smacking.

One of them burped loudly and the others laughed. That explained how he had got away from the wagons without being seen; they had pulled back to eat their meal, which had probably been cooked farther up the canyon. They were close enough to poke with a stick, and two were coming closer. Quickly, he slipped the sombrero and the pack off and held them in the same hand as his crossbow, then pulled his pistol and started up the trail toward the oncoming Indian. His hair was still tied with a bandana. The brave ahead of him was of medium size, shirtless, with the large breechcloth that characterized his people. He was carrying a small bow and a deerskin quiver, and was obviously intent on getting something to eat before his compadres ate it all.

They were no more than six feet apart now and the man said something to him. Swanson stayed in the middle of the trail and made the smaller man move over somewhat

62

as they passed. Hearing one of the Mexicans scream, Swanson mumbled the Mexican word for chicken, *pollo*. The man was a step or two past him. Swanson continued climbing, taking care not to hurry. He heard the Apache who had passed him repeat the word to the others and they laughed. Then one of them called something out to him, once, then louder a second time. '*Pollo*,' Swanson yelled back down to them and they laughed louder.

He sat on a giant flat-topped rock among the fractured boulders and magnificent cliffs of the canyon's rim until his adrenalin had stopped spurting. Then he pulled his telescope and looked out at the dark grey sea of desert that fell away a thousand feet below for as far as his eye could see. Fifty miles in the distance he made out the shape of a dark sawtoothed mountain. Patiently, he worked the circular lens over the desert landscape below, searching for a campfire, the flare of a match, a tent lantern ... anything that would mean white men and help. After twenty minutes, he could find nothing in the darkness below that indicated he was anything but alone. He put the telescope away and listened to the distant yapping of coyotes forming up for the night's hunt. He had been raised in the desert, it was his home, and yet on this night it felt alien and hostile to him, and he as lost and alone as ever in his life. He started walking.

The Apaches had been watering their stock at the spring where he had found the dead Mexican and the nun, and it was low and dirty now. He allowed himself to take a long drink and then he heard a noise. He limped into the bushes a few yards away and sat watching. It wasn't long before two Apaches brought four mules to drink at the pool. They seemed to be there for ever, the precious contents of the spring being noisily sucked up. It was a drip pool and would take a week to refill.

He needed that water. Swanson raised the crossbow and sighted on one of the Indians who leaned against a large rock a few yards away. His companion was squatting on his haunches in the sand talking in a low voice. Swanson guessed he'd have a fair chance of putting a bolt through the head of the standing Indian and reload before the second Apache became alarmed. As he figured the odds, the squatting Indian stood and yanked the lead rope on one of the mules and started them back up the trail the way they'd come. Swanson followed them until he found where they were holding the horses and mules, then returned to the spring. The mules had almost finished the water.

He was able to fill one of the canteens and half of the other before it ran out. When he was done, he took the bandana off his head and soaked up the remaining moisture in the pool and rubbed it over his face. It felt glorious. He wrapped the cool, damp cloth around his neck and then went back into the hills a few yards above the spring and found himself a place among the mesquite where the breeze was blowing into his face and he could sit down and still have a clear field of fire at anything that approached the pool.

He slipped a quarrel into the cocked crossbow and settled down to wait. He figured it wouldn't take long. And he was right. A grey fox came to the spring first. It licked at the wet rocks and then trotted off to find water elsewhere. Next came the javelinas he had heard earlier. The little pigs with their wiry hair were snarling and barking at each other, and breaking into squealing fights. He was aiming at the skull of a fat looking sow when he heard a mule deer snort. He waited. Venison steak would be even better. The big buck, grey against the night, walked in slowly, cautiously, scenting the air and snorting a couple more times at the smell of the javelinas. He dropped it where it stood at twenty-five yards with a brain shot.

Swanson took a hind quarter, the liver and some other choice cuts, wrapping them in the deer's own hide. He stood up and wiped the blade of his knife on his pants and then rubbed clean sand over his bloody arms. His thoughts were on California. He had enough food and water to make it to the next rain basin, and he could slip a horse out of the Apache's herd. Once there he could fill both canteens and the deer intestine with water and ride out.

Sister Elizabeth and Sister Martha were sitting side by side in the centre of the enclosure near the cold ashes of the cook fire. Sister Martha looked anxious, her eyes probing the dark shadows beyond the wagons, her hands clasped together in her lap. Sister Elizabeth was idly drawing patterns in the sand with a finger.

'I pray he is all right,' Sister Martha whispered.

'I know how much you believed in him,' Sister Elizabeth said gently. 'I'm sorry.' There was no victory in her voice.

'I don't believe he just left us. He had a reason.'

Sister Elizabeth smiled at her sympathetically and reached out for her hand. Sister Martha was trembling when she touched her and her skin was cold even in the heat of night.

She continued to stare off into the darkness beyond the

65

wagons. 'I wonder what it's like to die the way Sister Ruth died.'

Neither of them spoke for a few minutes, Sister Martha staring into the night and Sister Elizabeth watching her face and holding her hand. Then Martha said, 'Why would Jesus let Sister Ruth die like that?' She was sobbing softly now.

Sister Elizabeth moved closer to her and put her arm around her shoulders and squeezed. 'Do you remember how Father John used to say that the only difference between saints and the rest of us was that the saints had relived the passion and suffering of Christ? Had used the crucifixion of Christ as a model of how to die in agony even that they might have life?'

Sister Martha snuffed her nose and nodded her head in understanding.

'The Lord will help us accept the pain when the time comes,' Sister Elizabeth said bravely, 'and we will enter glory arm-in-arm.' They hugged each other. Sister Martha pulled back and held Sister Elizabeth at arm's length. She was smiling through her tears.

'I still believe Sister St Agnes,' she said. 'He was sent to save the children, and save them he will.'

The old nun sat a few yards away in the darker shadows under the cliffs, watching the two younger sisters. She prayed for them as much as she did for the children. They had come here because of her. So had Sister Ruth. She took her crucifix in both hands and began to pray again. 'Was I wrong about him, Lord? Was he not from You? In my heart I still believe he was and that he left for a reason known only to You, Lord.' She stopped praying and shuddered. The thought crossed her mind that perhaps he was the Antichrist come to weaken their faith in their moment of need. After all, he had killed men. Had she only selfishly wished him to be from God to deliver her from the burden of the children's suffering? The possibility was numbing, and she couldn't continue her prayer. All her life she had fought against her own headstrong will, had tried to humble herself before God. And now, in her hour of most pressing need, the moment she had lived and prepared for all of her life, had she failed her Lord? Could that have happened? Had the devil preyed on her frailties, her love for the children, and driven a wedge between her and God?

He had finished tying his things so that they would hang balanced over the bare back of the Indian pony and was ready to mount, when he saw her face again in his thoughts. The realization came to him, like a fist in the gut, that he could leave them, but he could never escape them. 'Damn,' he said, tipping his head into the horse's shoulder. The animal turned and looked at him.

Once or twice as he waited on the canyon rim Swanson heard the screams again, but they were weaker now, the end near. He held the telescope on the opening between the wagons. Inky darkness. Swanson started down. He had chosen the same trail he had sent the mule and the dead woman along. It ran down the middle of the canyon, closer to where he could still hear the screams, closer to the main body of Apaches.

He wondered if the dog had been shot or had finally taken it in its head to run off. It was about as reliable as wet powder and just as useless.

A few yards down the trail, he felt more than he heard

the faint sound of movement below him and he stepped quietly into the brush at the side of the trail. Seconds later, a bare-chested Apache materialized like a dream out of the night, trotting past him with a smooth effortless stride toward the rim of the canyon. Swanson blew his breath out and started down again.

The extreme volume of the next two screams startled him. It wasn't only that he was closer to them, their agony was greater now, laced with sheer terror. The Apaches had found a new device to extract pain from their victims' exhausted nerves. The sound had frozen Swanson in a crouch at the side of the trail, and as he straightened up he slipped the heavy pack he was carrying off his back and hid it behind a large rock a few feet into the creosote. He placed a smaller stone next to the edge of the trail where he would be able to easily spot it in a hurry. One of the Mexicans screamed again. And this time Swanson heard a woman's name. He started off in the direction of the sound.

Swanson knew from experience Apache camps weren't much and this one lived up to what he remembered. There were five or six cook fires and two crude brush huts. Those were unusual for a raiding party like this. Swanson figured one had been built as a death house for the wounded man he had gut shot and the other could have been for the head man or the bodies of the dead warriors. He moved the telescope slowly over the camp. A few Indians were sitting near one of the fires, eating. The lens came to rest on a large collection of fifteen or more warriors standing and sitting before two small fires that had been built under a fair-sized scrub oak. The source of the screaming was hanging upside down from the limbs of the oak.

With their arms dangling a foot above the ground, both Mexicans were naked and hung by leather thongs tied to their ankles. One of the men had a pink colour to him, and Swanson realized that he had been skinned alive. The other was covered with rivulets of blood where he had been slashed repeatedly with knives or razors. They had both been castrated. But that wasn't the worst of it. The worst of it was now. They were hanging over the two fires, their heads, shoulders and arms slowly baking. Every few minutes one of them would bend violently at the waist and scream out his horror, and then he would fall back thrashing over the fire below and the Indians would laugh. They would bake like that until their brains were cooked. Swanson turned away as one of the Apaches poked at the skinned Mexican's eyes with a red hot tip of a stick. The man screamed with pain and the Indians roared their approval.

Swanson would have preferred sighting on one of the Apaches, but he waited until both of the Mexicans had stopped thrashing for a moment, then he put a quarrel through the forehead of the man who had been blinded, hurriedly recocked the crossbow and then put the second Mexican out of his agony. As he recocked the weapon, he saw the Apaches staring in surprise at the quietly hanging corpses, not yet certain what had happened.

Swanson searched the crowd milling in the circle of firelight for the big leader. He couldn't see him. He did see the Indian who had gouged the Mexican's eye out with the hot poker. Swanson dropped him with a quarrel between his shoulder blades, then started running.

He ran past the small stone on the trail, then went back and found it and his pack. The weight and noise of what he carried made it impossible for him to run. He moved out at a brisk walk, trying to listen and peer ahead in the darkness. He could hear yelling from the direction of the Indian camp and knew that every Indian between him and the wagons was ready for him. He had no choice. They'd find him if he tried to hide, so he kept moving. He had a hundred yards to go.

Things went well until he reached the rocks of the river bottom and started across. Suddenly, three Apaches were on him. The first died with a quarrel through the chest and he got his knife into the side of the second, but the third hit him with a stone war club wrapped in deerhide and swung on a stick and leather thong. The force of the blow snapped the bone in his upper left arm, carrying him off of his feet and crashing on to his side in the rough rocks of the river. He bellowed. Still strapped in his heavy pack, one arm hanging useless at his side, the other pinned beneath him, Swanson was trapped like a turtle on his back. The Apache circled him cautiously. Swanson struggled to get his pistol out from under him, but it was no use. The Indian was coming in at him, his knife drawn. Swanson tensed his muscles, getting ready to deliver a kick, when out of the side of an eye he saw something fly through the air and land on the startled Apache.

Swanson had never been so glad to see the dog in all his life.

He rolled over on his side and struggled to his feet. The dog and the Indian were behind him, fighting in the shadows. Swanson charged with all his might up the rocky slope of the hill. The road and the wagons were a hundred

70

feet above him. He fell to his knees halfway up and heard the zipping sound of arrows beginning to fall around him. He drove hard with his legs in the soft sand of the hillside, clawing with his one good arm. He could hear them coming after him across the rocks below. They were gaining on him. He had two more yards to go to reach the road. His lungs were bursting. He couldn't drop the pack; inside were the water and the food.

The crossbow felt like a bag of wet sand, carrying it as he was in the hand of his broken arm, clutching his pistol in the other. He stopped and looked back over his head and saw five of them starting up the hill after him. They were coming fast. The dog roared through them, sending one sprawling, but the others kept coming. He sent a wild shot over his shoulder and then turned and began to scramble up the slope again. He lost his footing on a rock and, falling to his knees, he struggled to rise to his feet again in the loose sand and gravel, the hard breathing of the Apaches coming quickly closer. He felt the jolt of an arrow impact in the pack on his back. 'Bastards,' he yelled hoarsely. 'You sons-of-bitches . . .' For the first time he realized that he was going to lose, that he didn't have the physical stamina to make it. The thought was numbing. He had never thought of quitting anything and yet suddenly he felt overwhelmed and unable to move. He couldn't push with his legs. The weight of the pack seemed to pin him to the hillside.

Then the old nun was there above him, pulling him to his feet, tugging, dragging him up the slope. 'Mr Swanson – run!' Her voice seemed to energize him and he started moving again. They were on the road and lunging into the enclosure, the Apaches charging up the hill in pursuit.

He grabbed desperately for the Hawken, shook the

pack off and threw himself to his stomach beneath one of the wagons. He pulled the rifle to his shoulder with his good arm. Only able to move the butt of the weapon to sight, he missed the first dark head that came over the roadside but the explosion from the Hawken, followed by a shot from his revolver, convinced the Apaches it was foolish to keep coming.

When Swanson was certain they weren't going to try, he turned his head and looked around the enclosure. Sisters Elizabeth and Martha were sitting on the ground hugging one another. Sister St Agnes was standing in the middle of the sandy V smiling down on him.

'Hello, Mr Swanson,' she said. 'You're a welcome sight for these old eyes.' She was breathing hard.

'Thanks for the hand,' he mumbled and then a second later added, 'Ma'am, will you get down, please?' His eyes searched the rest of the area and then he looked at her and grinned. She grinned back at him.

A moment later, the pain hit and he pulled himself up slowly, grimacing, into a sitting position. Sister St Agnes saw the limp arm and dropped to her knees beside him.

'Mr Swanson, you're hurt.' She ran her hand expertly over his arm. 'Fortunately, it's a clean break.'

Swanson continued to look around the enclosure, biting his lip to fight the tears. 'If they handed me my head on a plate you'd say I was fortunate they gave it back to me.' He gritted his teeth against the pain.

She stood and went over to the wagons and returned carrying a small board and a bolt of cloth.

'I went for water,' he said.

She glanced quickly at him, then back to his arm. 'I know. Thank you.'

Something told him she knew the truth.

Sister St Agnes gave a sudden pull downward on the broken arm and Swanson let out a yell of pain.

'Don't move, Mr Swanson,' she ordered. She laid the board against the outside of the upper arm and began to wrap the cloth around the board, his arm and then his chest. Sisters Elizabeth and Martha helped her. He could see that while Sister Martha was smiling at him, she was also crying. Even Sister Elizabeth seemed glad to see him.

'I'm so happy you made it back safely,' Sister Martha whispered.

'Thanks,' he said between clenched teeth.

'I am, too,' said Sister Elizabeth. She avoided his eyes but the sentiment was genuine. Swanson nodded at her.

'Now, there,' the old nun said cheerfully, 'that's as pretty a set as you're going to see.' She tore the end of the cloth and tied off the wrapping. 'I'll bet you feel almost as good as new, don't you, Mr Swanson?'

'No,' he growled. 'I feel lousy.'

'Well, that's to be expected,' she said. 'You'll feel much better in the morning.'

'I think you just like to hurt people,' he muttered.

Swanson didn't say anything else. He sat staring at the sand. The three sisters sat in a semicircle in front of him, content to watch him and smile at him periodically. He was lost in his thoughts and the attention didn't bother him. Finally, Sister St Agnes cleared her throat politely. He glanced at her.

'Mr Swanson, the children could use a drink. If,' she added, 'you found any.'

He fumbled through the pack and hauled out the canteens.

Sister St Agnes stood and held out her hand, and Swanson gave her a canteen. She studied his face a moment, then said, 'Thank you for going for the water, Mr Swanson.' Her voice was gentle and reassuring. She watched his tired and dirty face for a few seconds longer. He was gazing off into the shadows. 'And thank you again for saving the children.' She turned and started toward the cave. The younger nuns got up and followed her.

'Make certain you drink some as well,' he said gruffly. 'Otherwise, your kidneys will stop.'

Sister Elizabeth had halted. 'May I get you some?'

He looked at her for a moment, then he shook his head and crawled off to the wall of rock and leaned his back against it, staring out into the night and thinking. He had to figure something out. Somehow he had to put a solution together. He leaned his head against the rocks. He felt lousy. His arm was killing him and the wound in his thigh felt no better. And while they had enough water to get them through another day, they could not stay here much longer if they hoped to get out alive. He had to cogitate a solution.

'Jaco has told the others that we should leave this place. That the women in the black robes are evil. Also . . .' The shaman was small and old, his skin wizened and wrinkled like the skin of lizard. He was dressed as a Gan, a mountain spirit, wearing a kilt, his body rubbed with ashes. A tall headgear tottered on his aged skull. They had fought and raided together for many years, were like father and son. The old man did not want to finish what he had started to

74

say. He stood staring down at the huge man sitting in the dirt next to a small cook fire hoping that the other would respond, but the big Indian would not let him stop, his stare penetrating, holding the eyes of the old shaman.

'And what else, Cadette?' the big Indian asked. 'What else does Jaco say?'

'That you should no longer lead,' the old shaman answered.

'And you, Cadette, what do you say?' the large Indian asked, his gaze now on the flames of the fire. 'Chato, Ponce, Ulzano, Chuchillo, Negra, all of you . . . what do you say?'

'I can't speak for the others,' Cadette said. 'For myself, I have followed your shadow for all these years and we have done well. That is what I say.'

Locan was the big Indian's name. He did not respond to the old man for many minutes. He sat staring into the fire, letting his mind wander over the events of the last few days and the years that had come before. He had never faced a challenge like this before. Jaco was no more than a drunken, vicious troublemaker. Nevertheless, what he said reflected at least in part the thoughts of the rest of them, otherwise Cadette would never have spoken the words.

Everything Locan had achieved for himself over the past twenty years of his life as a warrior was at risk now. All because of the black robes and the white man. While chieftainship was a birthright among the Mimbres, a war leader of prowess could win respect equal to any chief. And he, Locan, had proven himself in war and council, had earned himself a place of honour. He had been trained from youth by his father in the natural virtues of cunning and toughness. He had been taught, until it was second nature, that trickery ranked above pure courage.

75

Raiders who made off with a few horses or cattle and who were never seen were esteemed more than those who won greater bounty but suffered losses. And he had suffered many losses, enough to ruin his dream of becoming a great war chief of the Mimbres. He frowned, and the fierce countenance of overhung brows and out-thrust cheekbones made the old shaman take an involuntary step backwards.

'Jaco has a lust for Mexicans and women until he has to pay a price. Then his is the heart of a deer.'

Locan could feel the eyes of the old man on him. He knew he had said the wrong thing. He was their leader. He had to make a right decision for all of them, not attack in self defence one of his own, even if it was Jaco. He clenched his huge fists slowly in frustration. A war chief was not supposed to lose braves. Yet in less than three days, the white man who killed with the big rifle and another rifle that made no noise but fired deadly arrows great distances, had destroyed five of his warriors. Their dead bodies, painted yellow, black and vermilion and shrouded in their blankets, lay in the wickiup a few yards behind him.

When this was over he would take the dead back to the mountains, back to their loved ones, lead the first death horse and its warrior into the rancheria, hear the screams and moans of the women, and be stared at and shunned as if he himself had killed them. They would ask why Locan had let this happen. And he would have no good answer. None other than chance. Every man faces chance. But he knew in his heart that wasn't good enough. Jaco was a troublemaker but, then, Jaco had always been trouble and it had never come to this. No, it was not

Jaco's fault. What Jaco spoke the others felt. They were confused. Perhaps even afraid. They wanted to leave. They had the trade goods from the wagons, they had killed one of the black robes and three of the Mexicans. They had horses and mules stolen from ranches to the north. And in the way of nomads, they were homesick for the mountains they called home. They had been gone for more than thirty days ... sitting here for the last five. They were a patient people.

Locan sat up straighter and pulled the leather jacket he wore closer around him as if it were cold. Apaches could wait for weeks, but they should not have had to wait. They should have taken the wagons by now. They should have taken them on the road in the first assault but somehow the Mexicans in the lead wagon had struggled forward, up a hill and over the top, racing down out of control and crashing in the one place that gave them protection from attack from above. Was it the black robes' medicine? Jaco believed it was. Perhaps Cadette did also.

Locan rubbed the back of his neck with one of his big hands and looked up at the old shaman. The man returned his gaze without blinking. 'Tell Jaco and the others that they are free to leave. I stay here to finish the white man and the black robes.'

The old man watched his face for a few seconds before he spoke. 'You know they will not leave you. So you have not given them a choice.'

The old shaman was right; no Apache would leave his leader during a raid. 'I release them. I give them the right to choose.'

The old man watched him a while longer and then said, 'You give them no choice.'

77

He yelled and waved his arm fiercely, dismissing the old man. Locan let his eyes follow the shaman down the hill until he disappeared in the desert darkness. Then he looked back into the flames of the small fire. Did the women in black possess a powerful medicine? There was something to them that was different from anyone, white, Mexican or Apache, that he had ever known. They felt fear, that he knew. They bled, they cried out in pain, but they were not afraid the way other whites and Mexicans were afraid. They did not beg for their lives but they begged for the lives of others. He was certain that they were the spirit keepers of their kind. The one at the wagon by the water had pleaded for the life of the Mexican freighter, then gone quietly herself to a worse death at Jaco's hands. He rubbed his mouth in his hand. They prayed to their spirit god . . . they possessed a strange power. That he had heard.

Of one thing he was certain, the black robes were very lucky. They should have died of thirst two days ago and would have had not the lone white man suddenly appeared and sacrificed himself. And for what? Was he, too, from the mission of the black robes? Locan doubted it. Nor did he believe as the old shaman did that the man was a bad spirit. He believed that he was a fool. Nothing more. White men were like that. Fools. And, in an odd way, they were like the black-robed women . . . they would die for others they didn't know. An Apache would die for his family, a friend, even the tribe . . . but never for a stranger. Whites were fools, and this one would die for his foolishness.

Locan took some comfort from this thought, but it did not chase the vision of the five painted corpses from his mind. This white man knew how to kill and his dog was like a demon. It had attacked his braves close to the wagons and got one of them killed there and another badly wounded. Now he couldn't keep his men close to the wagons for a chance shot. The man was a good fighter. He would be hard to kill. But Locan knew this very fact was the only chance he had left to save himself from disgrace. A war chief who had lost five braves to one white warrior – a warrior who led nothing more than women and children against thirty Apache braves – was doomed to never again lead a war party. Was doomed to poverty and ridicule. The young men would not follow him. They would see him as weak, a poor leader, with bad medicine. Locan's one chance was to destroy the man, take the black robes, the children and the rest of the goods in the wagons. If he could do that he could claim victory over the evil medicine of the black robes and the spirit of the white man. It would be enough.

Locan stood and stretched his huge body. He would kill the man himself. He believed in the People of the Dreams and the godhead, Yusn. He would kill the man and then he would watch for a sign. His sign. A sign that would tell him how to survive the loss of five warriors.

Jaco was a woman, Locan thought.

Swanson was almost delirious from the pain in his arm and leg. He sat propped against the rock wall of the mountain staring out, without really seeing, into the dark-ness of the canyon. The old nun was curled up on a blanket a few yards away, asleep. The night was as hot as any he had ever felt in his life and mixed with the fever in his body; he was drenched with sweat and thirsty, but feeling too punk to move and he wasn't desperate enough to wake the old woman. Let her sleep in peace, he thought, it may be her last.

His mind began to wander over the events of the last couple of days, and he drifted in and out of consciousness. In his thoughts, he worked his way through his meeting with this old nun a hundred times. And he chewed on this thing she was asking of him. Each time, it came out the same: there was no figuring it. Swanson shook his head to clear it and focused his eyes on the wheel of the wagon. It made no sense. But then a lot of things hadn't made sense these past few days. The fact that he had been able to leave and enter the wagons without even being seen, let alone shot at, didn't make sense. It wasn't like Apaches to let their victims move around like that.

He let his eyes drift across the darkness of the enclosure to the darker outline of the old woman's back lying on the blanket. There, in the shadows in her black robes, she was almost invisible to the eye. Swanson studied the blotch of blackness until he could make her out. She looked small and childlike in her sleep. He continued to watch her for a few minutes and listen to the sounds of a night bird high in the rocks overhead.

Though he thought she was foolhardy, he had to admit she had grit in her craw. He smiled and shook his head. She was one of the luckiest people in the world. She'd come all the way from Pennsylvania to the border of Mexico and the New Mexico territory with two young gals who looked like they'd have a time of it finding the outhouse at a church supper. On top of that she'd carried ransom money on her without any weapons, other than her tongue, and then bargained seven kids out of the hands of a bunch of Mexican cut-throats. No mean feat.

She had hired freighters and wagons and taken them through two hundred miles of country filled with bandits and Indians before she ran into this bunch. Then her luck still held. The wagons had crashed into a place on the road with a rock overhang to keep the Apaches from tossing boulders down on them ... and as if that wasn't enough luck, there was the cave. It had kept them alive the two days before he arrived.

The smile left his face. He didn't like to think of himself as part of her luck. It came too close to her line about him being sent from God to save the children. He hadn't been sent anywhere, he had been hightailing it out of Texas to save his own hide. He stopped and pulled himself up straighter against the rocks. He remembered his dream of two nights before. A frown line formed around the edges of his mouth, and he looked away from the sleeping woman back out into the night and wondered what his life held for him, if anything, and what he could possibly do to save these people. Whatever it was, it wasn't much and it got less every day. He was holding his pistol in his lap and he was tense. The dog had not returned. He drifted into a fitful sleep.

He almost screamed when he awoke. Someone was putting something metallic into his mouth. He shoved it away violently and raised his pistol. The boy lay sprawled in the dirt on his back, wide-eyed and holding one of the canteens on his chest. When Swanson had recovered enough to speak he said, 'Son, that was dangerous. You could have been killed.'

The boy was trying to stand up on his bad leg and hold the canteen without spilling it. It was a struggle but he did it manfully. It was obvious that he was embarrassed and not sure of what to do. He turned and began to hobble toward the entrance to the cave. Swanson shook the final web of fright and delirium from his head. He realized he was still holding the cocked pistol on the boy. He lowered it and released the hammer.

'I could use that water,' he said, loud enough for the boy to hear but not loud enough to wake the old sister. Even so, she stirred on the blanket. The boy stopped walking. He was looking down at his bare feet, his back to Swanson. Slowly, he turned and came back, his head down, his shoulders dropped. He offered the canteen with both hands but didn't look into Swanson's face.

In the moonlight that reflected off the wall of the mountain, Swanson could see the boy's face clearly. It was the first time that he had seen it straight on and close up. It was worse than he had first thought. It had been done with dried pine needles tied to sticks and ignited. They burned with great intensity but only briefly, ensuring that the victim suffered but didn't die. It was the work of squaws. The disfigurement made Swanson want to turn away, but he forced himself to keep his eyes steady on the boy's face. Scar tissue was everywhere, almost closing one eye; a lump of it on one cheek seemed to pull one side of his mouth up in a permanent half snarl. One of his eyebrows had been burned off and an ear either cut or burned to a shrivelled mass of tissue. The result was a small face that made no sense when looked at. He wondered if the boy had seen himself in a mirror yet. He hoped not. There was time enough for that. Anger welled up in his chest against people who could do this to a child. He wondered how the old nun could call them God's children. The boy was still staring down at the ground.

Swanson pretended to take a long drink from the canteen and then offered it to the boy. He didn't move. 'Thanks,' Swanson said, corking the canteen. He waited a few seconds to see if the boy would speak. When he didn't, Swanson put the canteen back in the boy's hands.

The boy started toward the cave. 'I need some help out here,' Swanson said.

The boy turned and sat down a few feet from Swanson and looked out into the darkness.

'I need help to watch over things . . . someone to spell me. You willing?' The boy was listening, but his expression never changed and he continued to stare straight ahead.

When Swanson was convinced that the boy wasn't going to respond, he said, 'That's good.'

They sat without talking. Then Swanson drifted back into sleep. When he awoke some two hours later, the boy was still sitting there staring out at the night, holding Swanson's knife in his hand. Surprised, Swanson reached down and felt his empty sheath. 'When did you lift my knife,' he asked groggily. The boy didn't answer.

'That knife is big for you, but I have another that would suit you.' Swanson fished into the bag lying in the sand next to him and brought out a folding knife with a bone handle and tossed it over next to the boy. 'This one belonged to my brother. You're welcome to use it.'

The boy said nothing, nor did he look at the knife; he simply continued to sit there in the darkness. When Swanson was almost convinced that perhaps he was deaf in his near ear and had not heard him, he saw the boy's small hand reach out and pick the knife out of the sand and bring it to his lap.

'Don't let Sister St Agnes catch you with either one of those or she'll tan both our hides. Fact, give me the big one back.' He held his hand out toward the boy. Matthew continued to cradle both knives in his lap. Swanson let his hand drop.

'Where you from, boy? You Texan or New Mexican?'

He waited a few minutes to let the questions sink in, watching the boy's face for some expression. There was no visible response.

'If you want to go home again, you have to tell someone where you came from. Or who you are. Otherwise, no one will ever know and then how you going to get home?' Swanson couldn't tell whether the boy was even listening. His brown hair was matted and dirty. The few clothes the nuns were able to stitch together for him were girl things, they barely covered his backside and his small buttocks were visible in places. Something heavy rose in Swanson's chest as his mind worked back to the day when the Comanches slaughtered his family. He seldom did that any more.

It had happened on their place in the Texas panhandle in the fall of 1831. He had just turned eight. His mother was there, his father, his older brother, Joshua, and his little sister, Pearl. Joshua had turned thirteen a few months before and their father had given him an old .36 calibre flintlock. Swanson remembered that he thought Joshua was just about the biggest and best thing alive in the world.

The Comanche had come out of the plains sometime during the night. Afterwards, he always felt he had sensed their presence because he had awakened in the thick darkness of the dugout frightened and crying and his mother had crawled out of bed and come and comforted him. It was the last time she ever held him in her arms and fussed over him.

Swanson remembered how she had held him in her lap that night, rocking him in the old rocker, the treads making a quiet grating sound as they moved over the dirt floor. She had smoothed his hair and talked to him and, like always in her arms, listening to her warm voice, he had calmed down. After a while, his sister had started to fuss and his mother had kissed him and told him she loved him and then tucked him back in bed with Joshua. He had started to say he loved her too, but he never had been able to say that. And he never got the chance. It was one of two things in his life that he was sorry about. The other thing was that, try as he might, he couldn't remember what his mother's face looked like. He remembered she had dark hair. And sometimes when he was places where there were women, he heard a laugh that reminded him of her soft laughter. But he had lost her face. He used to try and remember it for hours on end. But it was no use. It was the only thing in life that made him want to cry.

That next morning, he had come full awake before dawn, sitting bolt upright in bed. His father was standing at the heavy door and squinting out through a gun hole. He stayed there most of the day, just watching, not letting any of them out. Then, near sundown, he had taken his rifle and said he had to water and feed the stock. He could still remember the strange sound in his mother's voice when she asked him not to go, but his father had said there was nothing to worry about.

They shot him near the stables and his mother had grabbed baby Pearl and run outside, yelling into the dugout for him to crawl into the hide-hole. Because of the sound in her voice he had done what she told him, grabbing the old crossbow and looking back as he slipped into the place in the wall behind his parents' bed in time to see Joshua dart out clutching his rifle. He had heard Joshua scream, followed by an awful sound that he knew was his mother's voice.

The Comanche raiders had been moving fast, probably pursued by territorials, and they never found where he was hiding. Days later, he had been picked up wandering in the desert. From that day until his fourteenth birthday, he had been raised by a string of people, none kin. He was more worker to them than family. Thinking back, he had hated that the most. Not the work, just the fact that he didn't mean anything to the folks he lived with. He had come to feel like a half-broken colt that was being ridden too hard. At fourteen, he decided he would work for himself. And he had done just that, working as a hand, an outrider for freighters, a scout and a range fighter. He had been home – schooled and the best thing he brought any employer was his fight. He didn't look for trouble . . . but he never looked away, either.

Swanson forced himself from his thoughts and glanced at the small boy sitting a few feet away from him. For all that passed between them, the boy might have been sitting alone in the middle of desert a thousand miles from another person. But Swanson understood.

'I was on my own, too, when I was your age,' he said. Swanson thought that he noticed the boy's head move slightly at the sound of his voice, but he couldn't be certain. 'But if you got kin, then you aren't alone.' He pulled his pack closer to him and fumbled through it and brought out his extra shirt. He tossed it to the boy.

'Put that on. It's big, but we can fix it.' The boy didn't move. 'We need to find out if you have kin.'

Locan had been near the wagons, listening to the man talk to the boy, for more than an hour. He lay stretched out in the sand, naked except for his breechcloth and soft boots, his hand sweating on the leather grip of the heavy short bow, his other hand clutching three arrows, more than enough to kill the white warrior. It would be over soon now. He was lying near one of the wheels, no more than ten feet from the gap between the wagons, no more than twenty-five feet from the man and the boy. There was no one else in the enclosure. The white man was not as good as he had at first thought. Either that or his wounds and the fatigue were taking their toll on him. He should have seen Locan moving like a snake over the ground long before now. Fortunately for Locan the dog was not there. Perhaps one of his men had truly killed it, as they had claimed to have done so many times during the past three days.

Locan was waiting for the man to tire again and to drift into sleep, as Locan had sensed he had done a couple of times before. He could not be certain because the boy and the man did not carry on a normal conversation; the boy never spoke. But Locan was close enough to be certain whenever the man next went to sleep. And when he slept again, Locan would strike. In the meantime, he would not stare directly into the man's eyes; he would visualize himself as nothing more than the sand and brush of the desert and the man would be powerless to see him. He had mastered this as a boy hunting mountain sheep with nothing more than a knife, had learned how to diminish physical self as he lay in ambush so that his prey would not suspect his presence. He let his mind expand and wander like smoke, making certain he did not focus his thoughts on the white warrior so the man would not sense his peril.

Below him, across the river of rocks, waited the little shaman, Cadette, and Locan's enemy, Jaco. They were the only two he had told of his plan. He knew Cadette was murmuring prayers to the Yusn and the Dream People and that his power was good. Jaco was probably drunk. It didn't matter. It would be enough that they were witness to his victory. Jaco the coward would blow it all out of proportion and make the simple killing of this white man into an heroic deed, and Cadette would lend credence to the act. It would be enough to save him from the disaster that surrounded and clutched at him. Nothing would bring back the dead warriors. But a struggle and victory over the evil spirits of the black robes and the white warrior would be sung in the rancherias of the Tci-he-nde Mimbre Apaches for many years. Locan smiled to himself and let his body move forward a finger's width over the sand. Then he relaxed his muscles, his breathing became shallow and infrequent, the beat of his heart slowed until he was lying so still that an hour later a rattlesnake moved over his arms and back without knowing he was alive.

A desert wind moved up the canyon blowing a hot, desiccating breath over Swanson. The old nun tossed under its touch but continued to sleep, and the boy, still sitting up, stared stoically ahead, although Swanson had seen his small body waiver unsteadily once a few minutes before. He had not touched the shirt. Slowly, Swanson shifted his body on the sand so that he was sitting straighter against the outcropping of rocks. Somewhere nearby in the darkness he sensed that something was moving. Perhaps it was nothing more than a coyote on the road or an owl soaring on the black drafts of the canyon night. Whatever it was, no nerve had yet gone off in his brain, and he continued to let his eyes and his mind drift idly in an attempt to forget the pain in his body. The sun had been down for more than five hours, but the heat still caused every pore to sweat. He wiped his brow and eyes with his bandana and focused his gaze momentarily on the faint outline of rock columns in the distance. He could not escape the dull sensation that something was moving. The vastness and the clear atmosphere of the high desert was deceptive to the eyes and made the gigantic limestone plateaux of the distant canyon wall, purplish blue in the moonless shadows, appear close enough for him to touch. But he was used to that sensation. Far above him on the towering cliffs something had disturbed a yellow-throated warbler and the little bird sent a shower of *wichity-wichity* cascading down the rocks. The air was scented with the sharp smell of creosote bush and flowering yucca.

Swanson continued to move his eyes over the rugged walls of the dark canyon and to listen. He wished the dog had returned. He had whistled for it three or four times, but it wouldn't come in. He was losing strength rapidly. The long days of strain, the wounds, the lack of sleep and shortage of water were coming home to roost. He figured at best, if he made no mistakes, no miscalculations, he could make it through the next day and still fight. After that, with no real rest and no water, he would decline quickly. From the pain in his lower back, he knew that he had already pushed his kidneys too hard. He concentrated his thoughts on escaping. There had to be a way. He wanted to go to California. He wanted to meet a woman. He wanted to ranch. He didn't want it to end here. He wanted life to continue.

And it could. All he had to do was leave. He could make it alone. These kids and nuns weren't his problem. They had gotten themselves in this mess. And yet they had become his problem. The kids never had a chance; fate had dealt them a bad hand the first time the Comanche caught them. Now the Apache had them. Maybe this only confirmed they weren't meant to get out alive.

He rubbed his hand through his hair and sat holding his head to try and stop it from throbbing. Was he going to die with a bunch of snake-bitten kids and three crazy women, he wondered. Was this it for him? Were his dreams as nothing? He let his hand drop to his side and watched as the boy tilted and then tipped on to the sand asleep. Swanson stopped struggling with his thoughts and felt better. Then he, too, drifted into a fitful sleep.

Sister St Agnes was not asleep. She also sensed that someone or something was nearby. At first, she thought that perhaps God had sent them help, but slowly she realized that whoever or whatever it was meant to harm them. She was not afraid. She continued to lie on her side and listen to the soft sounds of the canyon. She had never been outdoors much in her life, but in the days that she had been here she had grown to love this rugged canyon, its starkness, its reality, its beauty, its bare and simple relationship to God.

She knew the boy was a few yards behind her, and behind him, the man. From their heavy breathing, she knew both were sleeping deeply. Perhaps this was the end that God had planned for them. Perhaps they were to go quietly in their sleep. She wondered if she were meant to stop resisting, to sleep and let the Lord work His will. She said a brief prayer asking for guidance and strength and salvation for their souls. She tried to close her eyes again and sleep. She thought of the children and her dreams for their happiness. Those dreams had seemed so real and so right. Had she been wrong? Had she, once again, been forcing her will on the Lord?

Sister Martha was holding the sleeping Millie in her lap. The candle had burned down low and would go out in another hour and then the cave would be dark, day and night, until they left it. If they ever did. The thought of the darkness frightened her, and she trembled and felt the child in her arms move. She tried to calm herself. Sister Elizabeth was moving slowly among the children, praying over each one and affectionately combing their hair gently with her fingers.

Sister Martha looked down at the sleeping woman-child in her arms and wanted to cry. Beads of perspiration clustered on the girl's brow and Sister Martha dabbed them with a cloth in her hand. She had been so certain that the Lord had meant for the man to save the children, to give this one and her baby and the others another chance at love and life.

She looked up at Sister Elizabeth tenderly arranging the twins on their blanket and smiled. Then the thought came to her that perhaps the children had already received their gift of love when Sisters St Agnes and Elizabeth and

Ruth and she had come to ransom them. Perhaps God meant their four deaths – the deaths of four faithful servants – to stand as a tribute of His love for the children. The idea flowed warmly through her and she felt at peace for the first time since they had begun the journey. She realized now that they were not meant to leave this canyon, that their long trek and the struggles of the children were over. She understood with certainty that the man had not been sent to save them, though she wondered how he fitted in all of this. Sister Elizabeth had been right. He was fighting his own battle. She had seen the struggle growing inside him over the hours and felt sorry for him, saying a small prayer for his soul. Sister Elizabeth straightened up and looked at her and smiled. 'I love you,' she whispered.

Sister Martha's face was glowing with happiness.

Locan rose out of the sands in one slow, fluid motion until he was standing erect in the opening between the wagons. The boy stirred awake, his eyes wide, staring up at him in horror. Locan ignored him. His eyes fixed instead on the man who sat hunched over, his sleeping head resting on his knees. Locan knew the man was in deep sleep; he had been watching and listening to him for a long time now. But he was still holding a pistol in his hand and was therefore dangerous. Locan could not taunt him the way he wanted to, to repay him in kind for what he had done to him and the others. No, this would have to be finished quickly and efficiently. There could be no mistakes. The People of the Dreams did not favour men who made fools' mistakes. Locan notched an arrow on the string of the bow. The distance between him and the white warrior was no more than twenty feet. He did not have to move forward to ensure that he hit his target. He would drive the iron tip of his arrow deep into the skull of the white man and kill him instantly. Then he would deal with the black robes and the children. Locan's heartbeat quickened. The boy was stirring. He heard him mumbling frantically. Locan pulled his bow and began to take aim on the man. The boy sat up and struggled to crawl between him and the white man. The big Indian glared at him and stepped to the side so that he could see the sleeping man's head clearly again. The boy looked back at the man and yelled louder. The man didn't move. The boy tried to stand and thrust his hand out frantically between Locan and the white warrior. Locan pulled the bow with all his might and then, as he was sighting down the arrow, the very shadows of the enclosure seemed to explode before his eyes and a black robe suddenly materialized out of nothing between him and the white warrior and the boy, her arms outstretched, face wildly contorted, eyes blazing into his as if they could see into his darkest depth. No man and certainly no woman had ever looked at Locan in that manner. Startled, he drove the first arrow into her, and when she did not go down, he notched another and pulled the bow with all his strength and released a second into her. And still she did not fall, did not cry out, only looked at him with eyes that held his own as if in a trap. He glared at her with a half snarl of contempt and took his time notching the third arrow. He would put this arrow in the old black robe's face and see if she could still stand. Then, out of the side of one eye, he saw the man rising, his pistol coming up. Locan whirled and was gone in an instant in the darkness.

Swanson made it to Sister St Agnes' side just as she was sitting down in the sand. She was staring at the spot where the giant Indian had stood moments before, as though she expected him to return. She was breathing in shallow gulps. Swanson went down on his knees and supported her with his good arm.

'Ma'am,' he whispered. 'Ma'am?'

A few seconds later, she turned and looked at him and said, 'Mr Swanson, I'm so happy that you are unharmed.' She caught her breath, and then grinned. 'You've accused me of hurting you so many times that this time I really had to prevent it.'

Swanson tried to return her smile but couldn't. 'You did just that, ma'am, and I thank you.' He hesitated, watching her face. 'How do you feel?'

She blinked her eyes and raised her eyebrows and then smiled again. 'Mr Swanson, I am pleased to say that I feel fine.'

'No time to be heroic, ma'am. If he's hit an artery, we better get at it quick.'

'I appreciate your concern,' she said, straightening up and using both her hands to feel over her body. After a minute or two, she stopped moving her hands and put them behind her in the sand and she leaned back and smiled again. 'Mr Swanson, as surprising as it may be for us to believe, I'm not hurt anywhere.'

'With respect, Sister, that's impossible. I saw him fire an arrow directly into you. He was too close to miss.'

'I agree, but I don't feel any thing wrong.'

'I've seen that before. Men in battle lose hands and legs and don't even know it.' His face flushed red. 'We've got to look you over.'

She said, 'In that case, I would prefer to have Sisters Elizabeth and Martha assist me.' She started to get up and Swanson held on to her arms to steady her. He was surprised by the bird-like frailness of her limbs. He continued to support her as they walked to the opening in the cave. He left her there, and then remembered the boy and whirled around.

The child was sitting in the sand, watching out into the night. Swanson walked over and sat down beside him. The boy didn't look at him. He was wearing Swanson's shirt.

'You saved my life. You and the Sister.'

The boy didn't move, didn't answer him.

'You spoke,' Swanson said. 'That's what woke me up. I heard you calling me. You talked and saved my life. I'm obliged.'

The boy shifted on the sand but said nothing. Swanson stood and walked out near the wagons to make certain there were no other Apaches hiding in ambush. He whistled for the dog one more time. When he returned, Sister St Agnes had not returned and he began to pace in front of the cave's entrance. A few minutes later, he saw Sister Elizabeth's head poke out of the hole in the mountain followed by Sisters St Agnes and Martha. The old nun was grinning.

'The luck of Saint Patrick, have I. Not a scratch.'

'That's impossible.'

Sister St Agnes raised her arms high over her shoulders as if she were blessing the entire canyon and the two other nuns pulled her flowing robes out. 'We found two holes where the arrows passed through my habit but both missed me. My arms were outstretched. The Indian mistook me for a much heavier nun.' She chuckled.

'He may have thought he was shooting at me,' Sister Martha said shyly.

'Child,' the old nun chided.

Swanson looked at Sister Elizabeth, his face serious. 'You're certain? You checked her carefully?'

Sister Elizabeth nodded. Swanson walked over and examined the small tears in the heavy black material. He shook his head in disbelief. Apache boys were given bows when they were three years old, and from that time until they died they lived by the bow and arrow, hunted everything from lizards to men with them. They learned to shoot off the backs of running horses, from up in rocks, while lying in ambush half buried in sand. And anybody who had fought them knew they were deadly accurate with their bows at a distance up to a hundred feet. And yet this Apache, this giant of an Indian who Swanson knew was the leader, had missed the old nun with two arrows fired at a distance of no more than ten feet. Swanson shook his head again. The old nun continued to grin.

Swanson returned to his place against the rocks and sat down. He was dangerously weak and needed to rest. He had grown up in the desert and he knew he was close to that invisible boundary drawn by the sun, the sand, the heat, and the parched wind – a boundary that if crossed would cost a man his life. He had to be extremely careful now. He had to conserve what little water he had, to stay still, to breathe out of his nose and to keep his mouth shut to cut down on evaporation, to stay out of the sun and the harsh wind. And he needed to sleep. If he did these things well and was very careful, he might have one more chance at escape. Any mistake would be his last. His instincts told him to sleep. But more than sleep, he needed to think. Very few things over the past few days had made much sense to him, but this last one made the least sense of all. An Apache warrior out to kill didn't miss a target standing ten feet in front of him. Twice. This time it wasn't luck. The old woman was charmed. No matter what the odds, she always beat them. Time and time again. Hell, the chance of his even stumbling on them in the first place out here in the middle of nowhere – a good hundred miles from anybody – was staggering. But it had happened. He began to wonder if the three men who had chased him out of Texas had driven him here on purpose, to this lonely, forsaken place. This place of destiny. But that was too spooky. If he wasn't careful, he was going to end up talking like her, saying that he had been sent by God. He shook the thought off. He might be sent to hell some day. He hadn't been sent here.

Day Four...

_____

Morning came on the canyon quickly. It was bright and brassy and laden with heat. The day would be one more oppressive broiler in a long unbroken line of burning sand and rock. Swanson stood up, all wobbly, and tried to stretch out his body. He stopped, the pain in his arm and leg jerking at him with a claw-like grasp. The enclosure was empty. The old nun had taken the boy inside during the night. Swanson had told her it would be best if she kept them all inside. He knew they cried in the dark without the light of the candle, but the blackness and the cooler air would keep them alive longer. They had only enough water left for one or two swallows apiece. Swanson knew that without the dog the Apaches were closer to the wagons, were waiting for him to make a desperate try for water. He might get away with another trip to the spring, but he doubted it. He only had one good arm and, on top of that, his wounds had sapped his strength in a way he had not expected. His luck couldn't hold much longer with the Apaches. He had to do something. Without water, the children would never make it through tomorrow. The thought of the children dying of thirst while he sat by and watched seemed to rush at him like some crazed and vicious animal and he kicked it away.

He wanted to just sit and shut his eyes and rest, but he remembered the invisible boundary between survival and death. He fought the urge and made himself walk around the enclosure. There had to be a way out. He wasn't a quitter. He figured he had a slim chance to get the kids and the nuns out of the canyon at night. The problem was that as soon as the Apaches found they were not in the enclosure, they would hunt them down. And in the open, he would have no way to defend them. That was the part he hadn't been able to solve since he got here. He guessed that, at best, he would have two hours from the time they left the enclosure until the Indians knew they were gone. He grunted in frustration. They couldn't cover enough ground in two hours. He needed a seven-or eight-hour head start if he were to have any chance of outrunning them. He continued to walk in wide slow circles, each step unsure and excruciatingly painful. He steadied himself with a hand on one of the wagons.

Then he saw it.

The dog was on its side, lying close to the rocks, half under the wagon. Its eyes were shut and Swanson would have thought it simply asleep had its mouth not been open and its tongue lying dry and cracked in the dirt. Dried blood was caked on its shoulders and side. Swanson squatted down next to it and saw the blood trail where it had dragged its body through the sand along the road. Gamely it had tried to answer his whistles. 'Dog,' he said. The animal didn't move. Cautiously, Swanson reached the barrel of his pistol out and touched it against the side of the animal's head. In the best of times, the dog was dangerous. Hurt, it was likely to tear a hand off. It didn't respond to Swanson's prodding. Something somewhere deep inside Swanson tightened.

'Dog.' His voice was sharp and mean sounding.

The dog didn't respond. Swanson extended a hand and touched the side of its muzzle. The hair was coarse and wiry, and he realized that he had never touched the dog before. He stroked the animal's head for a few seconds, and when it still didn't move he came closer and began to run his eyes and hands over it. Its back had been broken by an arrow that had severed its spine above the last rib. Crippled, the Indians had held its head down – probably with a forked stick – and slit its abdomen open. Its entrails were hanging out, dry and caked with dirt where it had crawled over the hot sand. And they had castrated it. Then they had let it go, knowing it was going to die . . . and knowing it would crawl to reach him. They wanted it to reach him. The bastards.

He ran his hands gently over the rough fur, down the long, bony legs, over the rawboned back. Then his eyes caught a slight movement, a faint pulsing of an artery among the entrails. It was still alive.

Carefully, Swanson picked the dog up in his arms and carried its limp body into the shade of the mountain. He spread his saddle blanket out and then moved the dog on to it. Swanson hurriedly brought the deer intestine that contained a small amount of water he had rationed for himself from the larger supply. He sat down, propped the dog's head on his thigh and dripped water into its mouth. When he had done this a couple of times, the animal swallowed and tried to move its swollen tongue. Swanson sprinkled water on his handkerchief and laid the wet cloth over the exposed entrails. He gave the dog water until there was no more to give and then he gathered the animal into his lap and sat cross-legged, holding him like a too-big child in his arms. He stared out into the bright sunlight of the morning, rocking slowly and talking low.

'California's a different kind of land. There's plenty of water, plenty of green grass. Our place is next to the Pacific ocean. A cool place with breezes. We're going to have cattle. I've never seen you around cattle. You don't fuss with horses and mules, so I've no reason to believe you'll bother cows. If you do, I'll just shoot you dead.' He was stroking the dog's head slowly. 'We'll put up a barn and a small house. Nothing fancy, but the house will have a veranda where I can sit and watch the ocean and you can do what you do best, which is sleep.' Then the dog's head twisted and it took Swanson's hand in its mouth and bit down. But the bite wasn't hard and it let go and ran its swollen tongue over the back of his hand. Then it went limp.

Later that morning, Sister St Agnes crossed the enclosure and stood looking down at the man and the dog he held. The boy was sitting close to Swanson, holding on to one of the dog's paws. Neither the boy or the man looked up at her. They continued to stare out into the sunlight of the canyon. She studied the dog carefully and knew it was dead. She knelt down in front of Swanson and reached to take it out of his arms. He shook his head and gathered the dog closer to him. The boy held on as well.

'He's dead, Mr Swanson. Why don't you let me take him and get him ready to bury? He needs to be cleaned up and wrapped in cloth.'

Swanson shook his head again and continued to hold the dog.

He held the dog in his arms for the rest of the day, talking to it every so often. The boy had let go of it, but he continued to sit close by. Swanson told the dog things that he had never told it during all the long nights and days they had spent together over the years. And he wondered why. Why he had not shared something with it other than his food and water in all that time. The dog had always been a good listener, had done what was asked of it, had been smart enough to know when to avoid danger and when not. It had never spared itself for him. And yet he knew they were both exactly alike ... neither of them could bring themselves to being close to anyone, couldn't open up and show or know affection. It took death to bring them together. His mother had once told him that death was a great teacher and he had never understood. He did now.

He longed for just one campfire night with the dog alive and lying nearby listening to him. Just one. He would tell it things then. He would tell it what it had never known. He would tell the dog that it was the only friend he had ever had. Something in Swanson, a thing that had been a part of him somewhere, had died with the dog and he was afraid to admit it.

It was close to noon time when Sister St Agnes led the children and the other nuns out of the cave and into the brilliant sunlight and the great heat. All of them stood with their hands over their eyes for quite a while, squinting painfully through their fingers. The temperature was close to 110 degrees and still rising. It would top 115 degrees in the shade and hover closer to 125 near the ground and rocks. Swanson continued to sit in the far corner of the enclosure, holding the dead dog. The sisters lined the children up in the little strip of shade that bordered the edge of the mountainside. Almost immediately, the children began to sit down as if they were plants wilting in the intense heat of the sun. Their small faces were flushed and it was apparent that they were very weak. Sister Elizabeth looked concerned. Sister St Agnes was smiling and talking loudly, while Sister Martha busied herself helping the children to get comfortable.

'Sister St Agnes,' Sister Elizabeth called. The old nun stopped what she was doing and walked over to the younger nun.

'Yes, Sister?'

Sister Elizabeth kept her eyes focused on the faces of the children. There were tiny beads of moisture on her upper lip and her white skin was reddening. Her eyes, beautiful and large and shaded a soft springlike green, were sunk deep into her face and made her appear tired and ill. 'They won't last very long outside here in the heat. We should have them in the cave.'

Sister St Agnes turned and stared out past the wagons into the wide expanse of gaping canyon. The sky was a deep blue, cloudless and thick looking. She didn't turn to face the younger woman when she spoke. Her voice was calm. 'Sister, try to understand what I'm about to say . . .' Her voice trailed off as if she were lost in her thoughts. 'You've done all that you can for them.'

'I don't understand.'

Sister St Agnes looked across the enclosure at the man

and the boy and the dog. Sister Elizabeth cast a glance at them, then she looked back quickly at the side of the old woman's face. The realization of what Sister St Agnes meant began slowly to penetrate her mind. But she resisted it. She had spent every ounce of her energy and willpower over the past two months to get to the children, to take care of them, to shoulder their burdens and fears, to protect and succour them, that she could not stop thinking in those basic terms of survival and love.

'It's best for them,' Sister St Agnes said.

'Best for them to die? It's suicide.'

'It's not suicide. It's God's will.'

Sister Elizabeth shook her head almost violently. 'We don't know God's will.'

The old woman swayed as if she were about to fall, then she steadied herself and stood straighter. She had a thin, tight smile on her face. She was still watching the man. 'I know all too well, Sister, that we don't. But thank you for reminding me.'

'Then may Sister Martha and I take the children into the shelter?'

'No.' the old nun said gently. 'We will not let them die like animals hiding in a dark cave. These are God's children. If they are meant to die, then they will die in God's bright sunlight . . . in this day that God has made.'

'But they don't have to die.' Sister Elizabeth was crying softly now, her back to the children.

Sister St Agnes stepped close to her and wrapped her arms around her. Sister Elizabeth sobbed silently against her shoulder. 'Sister, it's over. We must face that fact and prepare for the end. We owe it to the children and to God. They must not go to heaven without whatever preparation we can give them.' Sister St Agnes was supporting the weight of the sobbing nun. 'Hush, child, you'll frighten them.'

Sister Elizabeth straightened up and wiped the tears from her face with the edge of her habit. She smiled at the old woman. 'I'm sorry. You're right. I will do whatever must be done.'

'I know you will, child.'

There was one canteen of water left, and before she handed it to the sisters the old nun carefully poured a quarter of it into an empty canteen and corked it tightly. She placed this in the shade near the rocks. Then the three sisters began to make their way down the line of exhausted children. At each one they would stop, and Sisters Elizabeth and Martha would pour out the same measure of water into a small silver chalice that Sister St Agnes used for the Eucharist, giving each about three swallows-worth. The children took it eagerly, their eyes searching the faces of the three women. After each had drunk, Sister St Agnes would kneel and place both her hands on the child's head and say a small prayer of thanksgiving. When they were done, there was a small amount of water remaining in the canteen. Sister Elizabeth offered it to the other two. Neither would accept it and she turned and poured it into the chalice and gave it to the pregnant girl.

'There now,' she said pleasantly, after the girl had finished drinking, 'we had almost forgotten to give your baby his drink.' The girl closed her eyes and lay back in the sand. Sister Elizabeth knelt beside her for a few moments, her hand on the girl's stomach. Then she stood and joined the other two women at the wagons.

'I wish there was a priest present,' Sister Martha said uncomfortably. Her chubby face was sunburned and wet with perspiration. She was breathing hard.

Sisters St Agnes and Elizabeth had spread a purple cloth of silk on a rock the height of the nun's knees. There was a small bottle of red wine and a crust of Mexican pan bread.

'We will do what we have to do. God understands.' Sister St Agnes was leafing through a small black book. She moved to a place in front of the children and then knelt before them. She looked over their faces and knew that she had made the right choice. They would not last long now. A few of them would be dead sometime during the night, perhaps sooner, and none would live through the following day. She was surprised and touched by how quiet and at peace with themselves they were. None were struggling against their fate. Though in pain and craving water, they suffered like small animals in a strangely composed silence.

When her gaze came to the boy they called Matthew, she saw that he was looking at the man and the dog. Then he put a hand down in the sand and struggled to stand up. When he had done this he turned and limped closer to the man. The twins, Betty and Nan, watched him and then they also stood up. Then the nine-year-old, Jessica, did the same. Then Millie, the pregnant girl, stood and the rest followed. Matthew had stopped in front of Swanson and the dead dog and he stood staring down at it for a few minutes, the children lining up in the hot sun behind him. The man did not look at the boy and the boy looked only at the dog. He reached down and touched one of its ears, and then he turned and limped in his awkward gait to a place in the shade. The old nun watched and fought her tears as each child struggled by the man and the dog, some only looking at it, some stopping to put a hand on the animal . . . none saying anything to the man. And yet each, themselves near death and caught in the torments of thirst, shared their love of the dog with him in a way that only children can. Only the child called Anna reached out and touched her hand to the man's face. He did not respond. When they had all returned to the shade, Sister St Agnes cleared her throat.

'Children,' she said, her voice firm but breaking some, 'I know you're hot and tired. But we need to learn a few things about God. It's very important. So I ask that you pay close attention to everything we say to you.'

A few of the children had curled up on the hot sand as if to sleep. Sister Martha started towards them but the old nun held up her hand.

'Let them rest.'

'We can't teach them everything.' Sister Elizabeth's voice was tinged with frustration. 'What good can we do?'

Sister St Agnes smiled understandingly. 'We will baptize them, conduct Holy Communion, and Extreme Unction.'

Both of the younger sisters were shocked. Sister Martha's eyes widened and her lips, which were beginning to crack and peel, parted in surprise.

'But we aren't priests. That's forbidden,' Sister Martha said worriedly. 'We can baptize them, but to conduct Holy Communion and Extreme Unction we must have a priest.'

'It's sacrilege,' Sister Elizabeth added.

'I don't believe God would deny these little ones the peace and love of the Holy Sacraments simply because we're not priests. But I understand your feelings. You shouldn't participate if you don't believe. That would be wrong. So let me do it. Let the sin – if it be a sin – be mine.'

Sister Elizabeth stepped forward. 'We don't have any water for the baptisms. What else can we use?'

'All baptism means is to purify, to cleanse spiritually,' Sister Martha said enthusiastically. 'Surely God will understand that we have no water.'

Sister St Agnes stood looking at the two younger nuns until her eyes began to fill with tears. She was biting at her lower lip. She took a handkerchief out and dabbed at her eyes. Then she looked at the two women and smiled a wide, joyful smile that exposed her two large front teeth.

'I love you both. And as sorry as I am that you are here, I am thankful that I have you with me. You are my strength, next to God.'

It was late afternoon when they finished administering the last of the Holy Eucharist to Matthew. Most of the children were sleeping fitfully now. Sister Martha had fainted an hour before and she was lying against the sandstone slope of the mountain. Sister St Agnes wiped the small chalice and filled it with the last of the wine, then pulled a small piece of the bread that she had saved from her pocket. Sister Elizabeth sat next to Sister Martha. All the children were lying down in the sweltering shade. Sister St Agnes spread the purple cloth carefully in front of the two nuns and then knelt unsteadily and placed the small chalice and the tiny bit of bread on it. She broke the bread into three very small pieces. The sun seemed to hammer like a fist down on to the back of her neck and shoulders. Both of the sisters had risen and were now kneeling in front of her, their hands cupped together in their laps. Sister St Agnes wondered how many times in her life she had taken the Holy Eucharist. It didn't matter. This time would be the most important because it would be her last. Her hands were trembling. She knew the others saw it . . . then she saw that theirs were shaking as well, and it was no longer important.

'Body of Christ . . .'

When the heat would not stop pounding on them, and the wind would not come up the canyon, when hope would not show itself in any form, they slept. Everyone but Sister St Agnes and Swanson. The old nun stood with difficulty, picked up the canteen from where she had placed it in the rocks and walked over to the man and the dead dog.

He had been sitting without a hat in the direct sun for the entire day and his face was badly burned and blistered, and his clothes were drenched with sweat. Most men would have died. But she knew in her heart that Nat Swanson wasn't most men. He was half delirious from dehydration, and when he finally looked up at her, there was no recognition in his blue eyes. He looked back down at the dog.

Sister St Agnes knelt in front of him and stared into his face, waiting for him to focus his thoughts.

'Mr Swanson,' she said, quietly but firmly. 'I need to speak with you.' She waited a few minutes for him to move, to show some sign of recognition, something that would let her know he was listening to her.

'Mr Swanson,' she said, more demandingly this time. His eyes did not waver. He looked as if he were peering into a window to hell.

'Mr Swanson. This is urgent. The end is almost here. We've given the last of the water to the children. They will begin to leave us tonight, I'm afraid. And by this time tomorrow, most of us will be gone.' She paused and waited for some indication he was listening. There was none.

Her parched throat hurt her to talk, but she had to continue. 'I've saved you a quarter of a canteen of water. It's not enough to keep the children alive any longer ... but ... it will keep you alive perhaps long enough to find where the Apaches' horses are. If you can get one, you might have a chance to make it.'

She waited again. But still there was nothing in his face to indicate that he had even heard her. 'You did your best for us. But there's no reason for you to die here. Sisters Elizabeth and Martha and I ... we have a reason, the children. And we have a place to go. The children do as well. But you are not ready, Mr Swanson. You have things to do, to see and resolve. You can't save us now. You never could have. I realize that. It was unfair of me to have put that burden on you. Forgive me.'

She set the canteen down on the sand in front of him and reached out and touched his hand. 'You're a brave man, Mr Swanson. And I can understand why God likes you so much. But you and He have a great deal to work out between yourselves before you're ready to meet face to face. Take the water and go while you still can.' She watched his face for a few minutes. 'Sometimes it is far easier to die, Mr Swanson, than it is to live.'

She stood up, her head spinning, and realized that she had finally plumbed the depth of her own strength. She could now only move if God held her up. She took a breath and started to turn and walk away and then, out of the corner of an eye, she saw him motion at her with his hand. He was waving her close to him. Fighting dizziness, she bent down close to his face.

'Yes, Mr Swanson, what is it?'

He took a moment to speak and when he was finally able to, she couldn't understand him through his hoarseness. She leaned closer.

'Do you have a pencil?' he whispered, the words scratching out of his throat.

Surprised, she stood and let the dizziness subside. She looked down at his face. He was watching her now. She nodded at him and then turned and walked in a wobbly circuit to where she had placed her travelling bag. Kneeling down, she fell forward and caught herself with both hands in the sand.

After she had handed him the pencil, he had simply taken it into his hand and then laid the hand in his lap as though it didn't belong to him.

'Is there something else?'

He shook his head no.

Locan's senses were numb. He climbed the thin, rocky trail that etched itself precariously along the side of the mountain, arrogantly refusing to look down into the deep chasm of jagged stone. A misstep would cost him his life, but fear of natural things had never bothered the Apache. What he feared were the faint intangibles . . . . the things he couldn't see but sensed . . . couldn't fight but hated . . . couldn't understand but must. He was leading a mule with the body of a dead warrior strapped on its back.

The climb was hard, but not something that Locan was

not used to and he did it effortlessly, yanking harshly at the mule whenever it hesitated. The dead man was named Carlana. Locan and he had been friends since they were boys. A Comanche by birth, Carlana had been taken as a child in a fight between the tribes and he had been cared for by all of the rancheria but never adopted by any single family. His had been a lonely, harsh life, without a mother's hand, without relatives, but he had never begged, never shrunk away from it. He had faced it straight on. The loneliness, the necessity to survive on his own, had given Carlana a hard, sharp edge that Locan had always respected. Carlana was the only man in the tribe who did not fear Locan. But the lack of fear did not spring from their friendship; it came instead from a deep wellspring of courage in the man. Death was not something Carlana had feared. But now it had him in its rough talons. Locan wondered if Carlana still laughed at it.

Locan had been Carlana's only friend and he alone would bury him. He would spare him the false tears and hollow wailing of people who had never cried for him while he was alive.

At a place higher in the mountain, the trail widened and off to the side there was an opening into the mountain itself. A passageway large enough for a man but not a mule; a passage into soaring vertical walls, massive boulders, great ledges and plateaux and darkly shaded sandstone. It was a wild and lonely place . . . a place that was right for the burial of a man who loved the desert wilderness and who had struggled with loneliness until it had become a vital part of him.

Locan stopped the mule and untied the leather thongs that held Carlana. The body was wrapped in a brightly coloured wool blanket that Locan's woman had made. He hoisted the dead warrior on to one shoulder, pulled out an old rifle that had been trussed up in the leather thongs and then climbed up some rocks to the opening in the mountain. It was flat sandstone at the entrance and Locan stopped for a moment, shifting the weight of the dead warrior, and turned to look out across the sand and shrubs that spilled endlessly below him. The late afternoon sun was spewing brilliant rays of light over the peaks and miles of mesas. In the far distance, the sawtoothed mountain lay like a giant brown lizard on the desert, its ribcage cut by canyons. Over all was cast the deep silence of the land. Locan stared at the scene for a few moments. It was a fitting resting place for Carlana.

He followed the passageway between the sheer cliffs of stone until he came to a deep gash in the wall. The opening was seven feet long and a couple of feet high, and it receded deep into the rock. It would be perfect.

He laid the blanketed burden on the trail. He knelt down beside it and loosened a piece of rawhide that had been wrapped around the blanket and the man's head. He pulled the cloth back so he could see his friend's face. Carlana had been dead for two days and looked stiff and changed. Locan studied the features for a few minutes and then he began to paint one half of the face blue, the other red. He was careful and painstaking in his work. And when he had finished, Carlana seemed as if he might only be sleeping. Locan felt sadness creeping up on him and he quickly cleaned his hands in the sand and then ran a rag over Carlana's old octagon-barrelled rifle. Locan checked it to be sure it was loaded, then he placed it under the blanket next to the dead warrior and tied the leather strings.

After he had pushed the body as far back into the rock crevice as he could, he began to fill the opening with stones. When he was done, every inch of the slash in the wall was perfectly filled with carefully fitted rocks of every size and shape. He had learned this skill as a boy from an old Indian who had lived two summers with the Mimbres. This man had belonged to a strange tribe far to the south, a tribe whose people ages before had built gigantic rock homes for their gods. Locan turned his back and leaned against the wall of the mountain.

'Carlana,' he said, speaking loudly to the soaring cliff walls that surrounded him, 'I have buried you in death. But I know that you live now among the creatures of the other world. As a friend, I ask you to talk to the People of the Dreams, to tell them of your death, of my plight, of the medicine of the black robes and the white warrior who destroyed your life. Tell them I go to sit and to wait until I have received their sign. Tell them that I am willing to sit until I die, if I receive no sign. Carlana,' he said, his deep voice rising plaintively, 'stand up for me with the gans of the mountains.'

Locan knew that this was his last chance. The black robe in the enclosure had humiliated him. Even Cadette was convinced that the medicine of the black robes was too great for Locan. If he did not destroy the black robes and the white man soon, he would be disgraced for ever.

Just before sundown, the high desert begins to rapidly change colours. And it was happening now. The landscape of white sand, rusty cliffs and dun-coloured vegetation was beginning to shade pink and blue as evening edged closer. But the heat didn't change. It clung to the stones and drifted in the air like some omnipotent being. The children were lying where the nuns had placed them, too weak to rise or struggle against the thirst that clawed at them. The three nuns sat together, propped against the rocks of the mountainside. They, too, were asleep. Only the boy among them was awake. He sat a few feet from the man, staring out at the canyon. The man was still holding the dog in his lap.

Mustering his strength, Swanson laid the dog down on the blanket and then stood up. His face was on fire, covered with large blisters and cracking skin. He ached deep inside the small of his back and he knew his kidneys were failing. The wagons began to float before his eyes and he bent and placed his hands on his knees until he felt better. He picked the canteen up and walked unsteadily to the end of the farthest wagon. The pain in his arm and the wound in his leg was agony. He stepped around to the tailgate and looked back at the enclosure. The boy was still awake, but he was not watching him. Swanson uncorked the canteen and took a small sip of the water. It was hot but it tasted wonderful. He waited a few minutes to let the liquid move through his body before he took another.

When he had finished half the water in the canteen, he recorked it and put it in the wagon. Then he waited. Slowly, his body responded. An hour later, he was strong enough to stand without getting light-headed, though his head pounded as if he had been kicked in the face by a horse. He pulled a shovel out of the wagon bed and walked back to the rocks at the foot of the mountainside. He selected a rock about the size of a wash basin and, straining, rolled it on its side. Then, kneeling, he began to dig with his one good arm. In a few minutes, he was exhausted but he kept at it.

The dog was wrapped in Swanson's saddle blanket when he laid him in the hole. He half wished the old nun were awake so she could say some words over it. He didn't know what to say. He sat for a long time staring at the mound under the blanket. Finally, he said, 'I'll miss you, dog.'

When the hole was filled up, he rolled the heavy stone back into place, and brushed the sand around it so it wasn't possible to know that the rock had ever been moved. Then he went closer to the edge of the mountain and pulled the deed and the pencil out of his pocket. He sat thinking for a while. When he was finished, he wrote: 'July – 1858. This deed belongs to my next of kin . . . if ever found. Nathaniel Swanson, Rancher.' He looked at the deed for a long time, then he folded it and laid it on the sand and covered it with a pyramid of small stones. This was the understood marking for a spot of importance in desert country. If anyone ever happened on this lonely place, they would see the pile of stones and know that nature had not built it. And they would find his deed. And perhaps they would someday find a next of kin. The thought gave him some small sense of satisfaction.

Swanson glanced at the boy as he walked past him. He hadn't moved in a long time and Swanson wondered what kept him up. He had willpower, Swanson would give him that. He stopped in front of the old nun. In the evening light, he did not cast a strong shadow, but it was enough to wake Sister St Agnes and she squinted at him and smiled weakly.

'I'm so glad you're going,' she whispered hoarsely.

'When you get to a church – any church – remember us to God. Especially, remember the children.'

'Get the children ready. I'm taking them out of here,' he said.

Locan sat at the opening to the mountain passageway and watched the last rays of the sun tinge the desert pink. He had not moved for over two hours. Strangely, he had experienced a deepening urge to stand and retrace his steps down the narrow passage, past the slash in the rocks where he had buried Carlana, to an outcropping of stone he had seen only in his mind's eye. The thing that bothered him most was that he had seen the vision of the rock from almost the very moment he had sat down. And, for that reason, he had resisted it. He had expected to sit through the night hours, perhaps through tomorrow, before a vision came to him. He continued to sit, frozen in his body.

When Locan could not free himself from the vision of the rock, when the beating of his heart had begun to build with anticipation, he stood and started down the passage. He was certain it was only his mind playing games and he chastised himself for being like a boy. But he would look. He would satisfy himself that there was no single stone sticking out of the sheer wall of the cliff like the one in his thoughts. Once he had proven this to himself, he could return and settle down for the wait.

As he passed by Carlana's grave, he ran a hand gently over the rocks in a silent greeting to his dead friend. The narrow trail rose steeply here and he bent forward and started the climb. Even for Locan's conditioned muscles, the incline was steep and difficult. He pushed hard, breaking into a dog trot, making his way up the sandy path. He was breathing hard when he reached the top of the trail. He stopped abruptly. A few yards ahead of him, at shoulder height, sticking out from the massive wall of solid rock, was the single stone of his vision. He began to tremble as his eyes slowly traced its lines. It was the same in every detail, in texture, in length, in hue. There could be no question. This was the stone of his mind picture. Carlana had reached the Other Side. He had pleaded his friend's situation successfully before the People of the Dreams . . . and they had given him their answer. But what did it mean?

Locan moved cautiously toward the stone that stuck straight out, perpendicular to the red rock of the cliff. It was pure white quartz. Almost the same size and shape as a horse's head. The stone was not rare but it was certainly dazzling, thrust as it was in the red rock, looking to all the world like the tip of a giant's spear stuck in the flesh of the mountain.

Locan stood gazing at it, not knowing what to make of it. Not understanding what it meant to him. He reached a trembling hand to touch it. The surface was glassy and cool to his fingers. He caressed it. His excitement was building. He put his hands on either side of the white rock and pulled. He jumped back. To his surprise, the stone had slid forward a few inches. His hands were shaking badly. He knew now that his answer was behind the stone. He waited until he had gathered enough courage to pull the stone out of the wall. Then he grasped it again and gave a strong pull. The stone slid as before, then it was free in his hands, too heavy to hold, and he bent and let it rest on the sand of the passageway. Facing the gods is never easy for a man, and Locan straightened up slowly and looked fearfully into the deep, dark pocket in the red stone. It was empty.

He was more puzzled than before. He looked at the glittering stone at his feet. It was beautiful. There was not a blemish in it. As he studied it with his eyes, he thought he heard a familiar sound and he looked up and recoiled. Water was bubbling out of the pocket in the cliff, spilling out as if it were being poured from a large gourd. Locan put both his hands in the clear liquid and then his head. It was icy cold. He took a long drink. It was wonderfully pure and sparkling. He let it spill on to his chest and his back and it cooled him luxuriously. Then, as quickly as it had come, it disappeared. Locan stood there mystified. His eyes ran over the drops of water on his arms, the damp sand at his feet. It had been real. But what did it mean? He had come for a sign. And water was it. Water was rare and precious in this land. Water was life. Water meant new birth. Was that the meaning? That out of the pangs of his travail, he would be born again, victorious? Or was it simpler than that? Did it only mean that water was to be his ally against the black robes and the white warrior? There was no question that they had to be almost out of water – and almost dead.

Still, Locan was not certain that he knew what the sign meant. All he knew was that he had been blessed with a sign from the People of the Dreams. That was powerful medicine and not to be ignored. He would return to Cadette and tell him of the sign. And then he would demand that the others renew their vigilance, their determination to destroy the black robes and the white warrior. Out of the sign, he drew a plan. He could not lose any more warriors. Therefore they would wait. Water would be their death. He would let the water destroy the black-robed witches and the man.

When she could talk again, Sister St Agnes said, 'Mr Swanson, I appreciate your courage. But there's no reason to make the children suffer more than they have to. Most are close to death. They can go quietly and in peace here. Out there' – she motioned beyond the wagons – 'they face pain and terror.' They were standing at the wagon now, looking back at the line of children lying unconscious on the sand. 'No,' she said to him through a salt ring that had formed around her mouth, 'we need to stay here. We have already made our peace with God. We aren't afraid.'

Swanson was only half listening to the old woman. His eyes were moving out over the canyon. He turned back. 'Ma'am, get them ready,' he said.

Only four of the children could stand on their own and they formed a wobbly little line next to the mountainside. Sisters Martha and Elizabeth were rubbing their legs and backs and trying to cheer them. A few of the children were whimpering but most were silent and dazed.

'Do you have any more of those black outfits?'

Sister St Agnes had been staring down at the sand. She looked up at his face. 'Mr Swanson, you told me you couldn't get the children out of here. Why are you doing this? Let us just make them as comfortable as we can.'

'Ma'am, the cloaks. Do you have any?'

She gazed into his face for a long while without speaking, without emotion. Then she turned and looked at the children. 'Our spare habits are in the travelling trunk.'

*

When Swanson was finished, he examined them. He was satisfied. Each of the older children who could stand was wearing a piece of torn black material over their head and back, and he had cut the material worn by the two younger sisters so they could carry a small child on their backs under the black cloth. It was the best he could do. If they stuck to the deeper shadows of the canyon the cloth would help keep them from being spotted . . . that was, if they didn't walk right into an Apache. Swanson's head whirled. There were a lot of ifs. If the children didn't cry, if the nuns could muster enough strength to carry a child and climb at the same time, if he could find the Apaches guarding the horses before they found him, if the drip hole had water . . . if . . .

He stopped himself from contemplating and focused on doing. He knew from long experience that contemplative men wound up dead in the desert long before men who took decisive action. The sister was wrong. If the children were going to die, they needed to die trying to live.

He walked over to the old nun. She had been watching him closely for the past few minutes. Her eyes were looking up into his face and she tried to smile.

'It will be the darkest part of the night in a little while. There's not more than a half moon, but we have to be done moving the children before it clears the top of the canyon.'

'Mr Swanson, you think you owe this to the children, but you're wrong. Wrong to put them through this. Wrong to make them suffer. To have them die frightened.'

'I owe it to me, ma'am.'

He went to the wagons, pulled out his telescope and carefully glassed the road where it snaked north away from the wagons. Sister St Agnes followed him wearily as if she might argue, but she didn't speak. Swanson picked up the Hawken and handed it to her.

'I won't shoot anyone.'

'I never figured you would. Just hold it. You stay here with Sister Martha and the boy while I take the rest out. Then I'll come back for you. The two of you make some noise, talk loudly, maybe argue to get them watching the wagons and listening to you.'

Locan's eyes were on Jaco, even though he was talking to the old man, Cadette. The warrior was small and perfectly formed. The skin of his round face was smooth and soft. The white miners in Tuscon called him Velvet. Jaco looked boyish, though he was thirty years old. He was squatting on the ground a few feet from where Locan sat, holding a bow and a parfleche of arrows. A few strands of the black robe's red hair were tied with a beaded string to his soft deerskin teguas. His large doe eyes stared for a brief moment without expression at the big Apache's face, then he looked away. Locan's eyes wandered boldly over the smaller man's face. He thought for a moment that he could detect disdain, but he wasn't certain. Jaco was too smart and too big a coward to challenge the Apache leader directly. The old shaman was standing a few feet away, his eyes focused on the sand.

'I don't know. There can be no doubt the sign came from the People of the Dreams,' Cadette said.

'It means water is my ally.'

'It may be so. But I cannot say. All I can say is that you have been contacted from the other side. Only you can determine the meaning.'

Locan stood up quickly. He was frustrated. The old man was playing games and Jaco was enjoying watching him squirm.

'I have told you what the sign means. We are to wait and let my ally kill them. The whites will die without water. It could mean nothing else. Water is Locan's ally.'

'Perhaps it is so.'

'Of course it is so.' His voice had risen and he caught himself. He continued to stare into Jaco's face. Among Apaches, the very act of staring was an insult. Jaco kept his eyes carefully away from Locan's angry gaze. 'Did you move the men up closer on the wagons, as I told you?'

'I am letting them eat their meal. Then I will move them forward.' The words were spoken matter-of-factly but there was veiled disrespect.

'You tell them of the sign that Locan has seen. And move them closer to the wagons. I want them in the rocks of the river. They hide in the hills like small children.'

Swanson took Sister Elizabeth behind the wagon and made her drink the last of the water. She refused at first, wanting to give it to the children.

'If you don't, you'll never make it to the top of the canyon carrying a kid. And if you don't make it, the kid doesn't make it.'

Sister Elizabeth drank.

After that Swanson struggled and cocked the crossbow with his one good arm as the three nuns knelt together in prayer. Then he hoisted the lightest of the two small girls, Bonnie, up on to Sister Elizabeth's back and Sisters St Agnes and Martha covered the child with Elizabeth's torn habit. Swanson swung the other, Anna, wide-eyed and frightened, on to his own back and waited while the nuns draped them in black. He could feel her little heart racing and she was trembling.

'Anna,' he whispered. 'I'm taking you home now.' The child clutched harder at his neck.

When the nuns had finished draping the material over them, he turned and looked at Sister St Agnes. 'Make a noise but not so much that they crawl up to investigate. Just keep them listening.'

She nodded. Sister Martha was standing close to her, staring sadly at the line of children.

'Go with God,' the old nun said.

Swanson glanced at her.

'Have a little faith, Mr Swanson.' Sister St Agnes' eyes twinkled somewhere deep behind the strain on her face.

Swanson nodded and started down the wagon. The pregnant girl, Millie, followed, then Jessica, then the twins, Betty and Nan. Sister Elizabeth, with Bonnie on her back, came last. She was moving unsteadily. Swanson stopped at the end of the wagon and went to her.

'Sister, you've got to keep up. We've got to move out of here like one animal. Do you understand?'

'Yes.'

Looking at her face in the shadows, Swanson could see that she was shaking. 'Scared?'

'I should say no, shouldn't I?'

'Why?'

She only shook her head.

'Well, are you or aren't you?' he asked.

'Yes,' she said.

'Me too.'

Before he left the enclosure, Swanson turned and looked

for the boy. He was sitting in the same place he had sat all day. Looking straight ahead and staring off into the darkness as if nothing were happening.

Once Sister St Agnes had explained to the children that this was a game of Chinese dragon where each had to stay close to the person in front and do exactly what that person did, they did it perfectly. Swanson moved them in a half crouch from the end of the wagon, up a few yards to a large boulder. He bunched them up behind the rock in the space between it and the mountain, and got them ready to move out. The next hundred yards would be the most dangerous. They would still be in the side vision of any Indian watching the wagons, and they would be moving over the open road with only the light-coloured sandstone cliffs behind them.

When they were ready, Swanson picked up a rock and tossed it into the enclosure. Immediately, he heard Sister St Agnes say something loud and unpleasant sounding. He started out quickly, crouched, not running but moving smartly. At fifty yards, he halted and sank to his knees to let the children and Sister Elizabeth catch their breath. His arm and leg were throbbing. As badly as he wanted to be across this opening, he knew if he pushed too hard he might start one of them crying. He waited. Then they were moving again and across the last of the open road.

The desert silence seemed to magnify the children's heavy breathing to the point where Swanson expected to be discovered at any moment. He let them rest again at the head of a small trail that went off the road, down and across the rocks of the dry stream bed, and then began the steep, winding climb to the top of the chaparral. His heart fell. The canyon wall looked steep in the night air and the children seemed exhausted as they huddled together, panting.

'There's water at the top,' he whispered to them. He moved back to Sister Elizabeth. She was squatting with her head between her knees. 'Sister, can you make it?'

She nodded, still keeping her head down. Then he heard her retch the water she had drunk. He kicked himself for not giving it to her sooner. When her body had stopped its involuntary heaving, she looked up at him and tried to smile.

'I told you to give it to the children,' she said.

They were moving again. Down the slope of the hill, across the rocks of the river bed; suddenly a stone clattered beneath their feet, and Swanson halted them and they huddled like large black mud clods against the stones. When no Indian appeared to investigate, Swanson started them moving again. Across the river they scurried, then up the inclined trail that climbed towards the canyon rim. When they were a few yards into the chaparral, he stopped them again. The pregnant girl was gasping wildly for breath. Swanson put a hand on her thin shoulder as he moved past her in the dark. He stopped beside Sister Elizabeth.

'Sister, keep them here until I come back. Move off the trail a few feet and sit absolutely quiet.' He took the nun by the arm. 'Sister, there may be Indians passing by on this trail. Don't let the children move or make a sound.' She nodded.

Swanson eased the girl off his back and handed her to the nun. Anna tried to cling to him. 'I'll be back,' he said to the child. 'Then we can start home.' Anna looked into his eyes. She was sweating and panting hard. 'I promise,' he said.

Swanson moved up the trail a few yards to be away from the sounds of the children, to listen to the night, to listen for talking, the clicking of metal against metal, the sound of a cup against stone. He could hear nothing. He went up the trail almost halfway to the canyon rim and could see no one in the dim shadows. He smiled inside. The old nun's luck continued to hold. The Indians seemed to have pulled in tighter on the wagons, leaving the periphery of the canyon less guarded.

Swanson was squatting in the brush by the side of the trail, catching his breath, when three Indians passed by. They were trotting down the trail. Swanson's heart began to bump against his chest. They were headed straight towards the spot where Sister Elizabeth and the children were waiting. 'Don't move . . . Don't move . . .' he kept repeating between clenched teeth. He counted to ten after the warriors went by to give them enough lead time so they wouldn't hear him behind them, then he started at a jog after them. He could see the shadowy figure of the last Indian fifty feet ahead of him. His muscles tensed. They were close to the children now. Then they were by them and Swanson let his breath out long and hard.

When he reached out and touched Sister Elizabeth in the dark, she almost screamed.

'It's me. I'm sorry.'

'Mr Swanson, they were here. Three of them came by. I thought they had killed you.'

He nodded. Anna was curled up asleep on the sand. She looked exhausted. He picked her up as gently as he could with his good arm. 'Let's get going.'

It took them over an hour, stopping every few yards to rest the children, to make it halfway up the mountain slope. They were resting off the trail a few feet while Swanson, cradling the child in one arm, studied a narrow bridge of sand where the trail crossed over a washout. He didn't like it. The trail was all white sand here with no brush to hide their movement. He walked away from the children and listened. He studied the creosote bushes on the other side. There were boulders the size of a large barn fifty yards to the left. He let his eyes move over them. Nothing.

He set Anna softly on the ground. She tried to lie down. Sister Elizabeth held her hand, not letting her sleep.

'Let me go across first,' he whispered. 'If there's any trouble, I'll fire my pistol and take off for the rim. They'll follow me. You take the children off the trail to the right and climb through the brush to the top of the rim. It'll take you longer . . . but you'll be able to make it.'

'And you?'

'Hide up on the rim. I'll find you.' He knew it was a lie.

Swanson moved across the narrow neck of sand without incident. He positioned himself next to a large rock at the side of the trail and waved the rest across. Millie, the pregnant girl, came first. Then the twins. Then Jessica. He tensed as they came, their every movement clearly visible against the whiteness of the sand.

Sister Elizabeth started across leading Bonnie and Anna by the hands. Swanson saw the little girl stumble over the large rock at the edge of the steep incline and knew it wouldn't hold; she went down, pulling Sister Elizabeth off balance. The nun yanked the child up as the rock rolled down the steep bank and crashed noisily at the bottom. The sound reverberated loudly through the hills. Sister Elizabeth had pulled both children into her as she fell forward; she was hunched over, motionless on the exposed strand of sandy bridge. Swanson heard the click of metal and knew that a musket's hammer had been cocked somewhere nearby. He pulled the crossbow into his shoulder and let his eyes scan the brush. Then, out of the corner of his eye, Swanson saw him. The Apache was standing on the top of the largest boulder, holding a musket, searching the chaparral and the trail below for whatever it was that had made the rock fall. He had not yet spotted the nun and the children. Swanson was raising the crossbow to fire when the Indian said something and he saw the heads and shoulders of two more warriors rise against the night sky.

Swanson looked back at the nun. She was frozen into a tight ball on the trail, but it would be only a matter of seconds until she was spotted. Then, Swanson heard the loud snort of a desert mule deer. He moved his eyes to see the creature, but couldn't locate it. He was watching Sister Elizabeth when he heard the sound of the deer again, and, with surprise, he realized that the nun had made the snorting sound.

One of the Indians laughed and another said something and the three of them disappeared. Immediately Sister Elizabeth rose, the children in tow, and hurried across the bridge to where Swanson and the others waited.

'Close,' she said.

Swanson gazed at the strong features of her face rimmed in the white band of the habit. 'Where did you learn to do that?' he asked, his voice filled with admiration.

'I grew up on a farm in Minnesota. I figured whitetail deer must snort like deer down here.'

He watched her handsome face a while longer and then looked away. These women were a puzzlement. Every time he felt he understood them, they changed and he was as lost as before. He never felt that way about women in general. Women had always chased him. And he had understood them. What they needed and wanted. But these three women, he wasn't even close to figuring.

Swanson himself was unsteady on his feet and his mouth was dry and his throat burned for water. He didn't want to think how the children felt. He had left them and Sister Elizabeth hidden in some rocks on the rim of the canyon while he went ahead to find the Apaches' horses. The drip hole contained enough cloudy water to fill the canteens and one of the deer intestines and these were cached nearby in the brush. He had not allowed himself to drink. He couldn't afford cramps. He stood in head-tall manzanita looking and listening for the herd.

A few feet away in the dark, he heard a horse cough. The animal had probably been eating too much rough chaparral brush. Swanson went slowly to his knees and tipped forward on his one good arm. Painfully, he crawled out of the brush and down a small outcropping of rocks in amongst the horses. One animal snorted at him and whirled away. Swanson stopped and let them get accustomed to him. Most were Indian ponies or stock off New Mexico ranches and used to men, but not men crawling on the ground. A little black mare was pawing the sand at Swanson. She snorted and backed away. A small circle of horses stood looking down at him. He reached a hand up towards a horse and the animal put its nose out timidly towards him and then tossed its head and shied away.

Swanson tensed. Something had changed in the way the animals were moving. The herd was agitated now.

Something was wrong. Swanson could feel the animals moving in waves that were not normal for a grazing herd. Then he saw the Apache. The man was standing in the herd a few yards from Swanson, and in the darkness he could vaguely see the Indian's legs beneath the animals' stomachs. From the way the man was turning and standing in one place, Swanson could tell he was searching for whatever it was that had disturbed the horses. Quietly, Swanson turned and started to slip away. Then he saw the teguas of the second Apache standing behind and above him on the rocks at the edge of the manzanitas. They had him boxed between them. He had his pistol, but if he used it, there might be other Apaches within hearing. His one chance was the outcropping of stone on which the warrior stood.

Swanson edged slowly toward it, holding on to a small rawhide lariat that hung on the neck of a small dun. He worked a half-hitch on to the horse's mouth and then crouched under the animal's neck and guided him towards the Apache on the rocks. Sweat began to pour down his back. Slowing the dun, he turned to get a fix on the position of the Indian in the herd. The man was working his way towards him. No more than two yards' distance separated them. The old feeling stole up on Swanson again, the way it always did when danger was near. His breathing quickened, blood seemed to pound in his temples, involuntarily his muscles began to tense and twitch with anticipation. And, last, his stomach seemed to go hollow as if somehow it had drained itself of food and water and filled instead with fear. He was not a man to deny fear.

He moved the dun closer to the rocks and the waiting

warrior. The night was still and he wished for wind that would whip up the herd some, but none came. He could hear mosquitos from the drip hole buzzing through the night air. Two horses stood between him and the ledge. Through the darkness he could barely make out what appeared to be a narrow shelf in the rocks. He looked back over his shoulder. The Apache behind him was pushing his way steadily forward through the herd. One of the Indians spoke and Swanson used the sound as cover to crawl quickly under the bellies of the two horses. Startled, one of the animals cow-kicked at him, but he was already stretching out on the shelf under the rocks.

The Indian in the herd kept coming. Swanson wedged himself as far back into the shadows as he could go. He was almost completely covered but only almost, for the brim of his sombrero stuck out a few inches where he had stuffed it, as did the toes of his boots. He sucked his breath in and pushed with all his might into the stones. A rock gave way and then, a moment later, he felt a creepy, crawling sensation on his back. The awful feeling seemed to spread rapidly out in all directions, up his back, down his legs, on to his neck, over his stomach. The urge to roll out of the rocks was overwhelming, but just as it peaked Swanson saw the legs of the Apache standing a foot in front of his face.

Swanson's skin tingled and crawled as hundreds of small appendages scratched over him. He knew what he had done and the realization made his muscles twitch. He had broken the rock cover off of a nest of poisonous centipedes, and at least five of them were on him. The hair on his neck rose. One of the insects had reached the collar of his shirt and was crawling down inside.

Another of the angry insects worked its way into his pants and scurried over his thigh.

Swanson almost yelled out as the perforated head claws of the centipede on his back sank in, sending a surge of poison and a jolt of pain walloping into his back. He felt like he'd been kicked. For a second, it was hard to breathe. The Apaches were talking quietly. Swanson forced himself to focus his eyes on the stout legs of the warrior in front of him. From the heavy feel of the insects, Swanson guessed they were easily four inches long. He shuddered at the thought. Then the one on his thigh stung him and he bit his lip until it bled. Tears were flowing freely out of his eyes and his nose was draining mucus.

He was bitten twice more before the two Indians moved off. Swanson waited in the ledge under the rocks until he heard the Apaches talking on a small rise overlooking the herd. The bites were swelling and burning badly as Swanson undressed and shook the centipedes out of his clothing, smashing each one with a rock. He wouldn't die but he'd hurt for a few days.

The two young Apaches were sitting next to a small cook fire. Swanson could see their silhouettes clearly, and the flames waving gently on the sandstone walls of the small bluff behind them. He could hear them talking. The fire would be their undoing. They had been here guarding the herd for too long, sitting and doing nothing. Boredom had set in. Herd watch inside the Apache's homeland was a tedious duty left to the younger, less experienced warriors. And these two were inexperienced. For both of them to be sitting close to a campfire meant that their eyes would be blind to the night and that they would have only their ears to guard the herd. That would not be enough with Nat Swanson. They were lucky he meant them no harm.

He let them settle into their conversation again and let the effects of the centipede bites lessen some, then he moved slowly to the edge of the hill and quietly worked loose the stakes of scrub oak and brush that the Indians were using as a gate to block the narrow mouth of the canyon corral. The horses watched him but caused no more problems. One at a time, he slipped two ponies and two mules through the opening and led them down the long draw for a quarter of a mile. When he figured it was safe, he put a half-hitch on one of the Indian ponies and, leading the other three, mounted and trotted back to the drip hole, the dead Mexican and the third wagon.

The mules were well-trained animals, broken to harness. He guessed they had been part of the freighting teams. The two horses were half-wild range animals, barely broken to ride and afraid of both the harness and the wagon, so he hooked them up first, and put the two mules in the lead. The mules would hold the horses steady and could be handled. All four animals seemed in good condition and were rested. They were a little lean in the ribs, but tough enough to make it to the fort. If . . . if they had enough lead time.

Swanson let the children have one of the canteens of water. They were huddled on a small bluff above the canyon rim. And he sat away from them a few yards and watched the main trail on the rim of the canyon. He had backed the wagon into an open place off the trail, but he knew it could be found easily. He glanced at Sister Elizabeth as she gave each of the children a small drink of water from the canteen. She looked at him across the darkness and he made a motion for her to drink. She did. One small gulp. She was learning. She held the canteen towards him. He shook his head.

Ten minutes later, Sister Elizabeth had given the children two more swallows. Swanson stood and walked to the far edge of the bluff and stared out at the black sea of desert below him. On the far horizon, he could barely make out a smudge of light and knew that the moon would be up in a minute. That meant that he had no more than twenty minutes left to get the two nuns and the boy back here, and to get all of them into the wagon . . . *if* he was to have any chance of getting them out. There was that word again.

Swanson handed the children up to the nun in the back of the wagon. His heart jumped. He had only counted five. One was missing. He turned around quickly and searched the shadows. Then he looked back into the wagon and counted again. Five. Anna was missing. He looked up at the nun and started to speak, and she stared at him and shook her head.

They stood at the mule's side. 'Where is she?'

'With God.'

'What?'

The nun watched his face and nodded slowly.

'Why didn't you tell me?'

'There was no time. You did your very best. She went quietly. I'm sorry.'

'Did you bury her?'

'I said a prayer over her. She's at peace.'

'But you didn't bury her?'

'I couldn't.'

Swanson turned and gazed out into the darkness, remembering the little girl and the flowers she had brought him. His chest felt like someone was squeezing him. 'People have to be buried out here,' he said, as if talking to himself. 'Otherwise the scavengers and the Indians will get them.'

The boy saw him first when he crawled into the enclosure. Swanson motioned him over. The two nuns were asleep against the rocks. Something pulled hard inside him. Were they were asleep? He watched them long enough to see they were both breathing.

After the boy had taken a drink, Swanson took one and then crawled over and woke the old nun.

'You made it,' she rasped. 'Are the children and Sister Elizabeth safe?'

He watched her take a drink from the intestine, pulling it away from her when she had had enough.

'Anna is dead. The others are waiting for you in a wagon.'

The old nun looked away. He heard her whispering a prayer. He woke Sister Martha and gave her a small drink. Then he went back to the boy. He got down on his hands and knees and said, 'Crawl up.' The boy did.

They made it to the rim of the canyon just as the moon crested the palisades of stone, and Swanson once again marvelled at the old woman's luck. They scurried on like three black dreams moving along the canyon's rim. Then they were at the wagon and the sisters were hugging each other and the children. Swanson helped Sister Martha up into the bed of the wagon and Sisters Elizabeth and St

Agnes on to the wagon seat. He handed Sister Elizabeth the reins.

After he had led the mules in a half circle to get them pointed the right way down the trail, he stopped them and walked back to the side of the wagon box.

'Don't worry about resting the animals. The trail out of the mountains is all downhill from here. You know how to use the wagon brake, right?' Sister Elizabeth was watching his face closely. She nodded. Sister St Agnes was staring straight ahead, her lips pressed together in a tight smile that was no smile. 'Don't try and find them water either. They can go all night and part of the morning. There's a big water hole – an all-season spring – about ten miles out on the desert. You should hit it about dawn. Don't worry about missing it. You'll never get these animals to go past it.' He looked up at her and grinned. 'You sure you can drive one of these things?'

Sister Elizabeth nodded again. The old nun still had not turned to look at him.

'Good. Then just stay on the trail. And, whatever else you do, don't unharness this team. You'll never get those ponies back in, if you do.'

Sister St Agnes suddenly turned her face towards him and for the first time since the day, four days ago, when he had first met her, she seemed truly angry.

'So this is it. This is the way you get the children out without the Apaches catching us. You sacrifice yourself.' She stared harder into his eyes. 'Why didn't you ask me?'

'I'll keep them listening to my singing until just before dawn. That should half kill them. Then I'll slip out. It's no big deal. That'll give you a nine-hour lead. They'll never catch you. They won't even try.'

'You should have asked me,' she said, turning and looking straight ahead again.

Swanson saw that tears were running down Sister Elizabeth's cheeks. 'Go with God, Mr Swanson,' she said.

He nodded and walked past the wagon, raising his hand and running his fingers through the boy's hair as he passed. The wagon was moving down the trail now. Sister Martha and the children were watching him, all but the boy who sat looking out at the black vacuum of air over the canyon. Sister Elizabeth glanced over her shoulder at him once. The old nun didn't turn around.

Swanson found Anna's body on a small sand hill near where he had left them earlier. Sister Elizabeth had wrapped the child carefully in her undergarments. Her little hands were folded together. Never before had a corpse looked so alive to him. He wanted to shake her gently and awaken her.

He scraped her grave in the sand with his one good arm. His fingers were cracked and bleeding when he finished. He knelt over the child's body and felt bad that he hadn't got them out of the canyon sooner. That she would never see her mother. He reached down and touched a corner of the white garment. Then he stood up and walked off into the dark. When he returned, he was carrying a small bunch of desert lilac. He knelt down and slipped these into the small hands.

'I'm sorry,' he said. Then a while later, he rocked back on his boots and looked up at the sky. He fought the tightening in his throat.

'Dog. Stay with her.'

He stayed by the grave for a while and then slowly he

forced himself away. He had to try to save the others. As he stumbled along the main trail on the rim of the canyon, he gradually formed a thought that had been half-submerged in his mind for days. He shook it off. Then he stopped walking.

There was no noise in the night. He turned slowly in a circle, letting his eyes search the sand and the cliffs. He felt numb. The ground was smooth where he stood. The vague, gnawing thought was there again. If he failed, if he died and the Apaches caught the wagon, it would be as if nothing had happened here, as if none of them had ever stood in the deep sands of these ancient hills. But that was impossible. He had stood here. He and the old nun, the other sisters and the children, had stood here. They had fought here, cried and laughed. And the dog and Anna had died here. But none of that would matter, there would be no trace of their meeting, except for cold, metallic memories rusting in the sands. It would be as if none of them had existed at this moment in time. The thought made him shake somewhere deep inside.

Later, he had moved in a dazed walk down the canyon trail, surprising a warrior standing in the shadows near the river bed. The startled Indian had taken a half-hearted shot at him with his bow, then scurried away into the night. They were afraid of him. He did not know why. Nor did he much care. His thoughts were on the old woman.

He sat down in the sand of the enclosure. Immediately the fatigue and the pain of his wounds pounced on him, and he lost consciousness for a few minutes. When he awoke, he forced himself to stand and to move to the wagons. He took the shovel out of the bed and banged it a

142

couple of times on the wheel. Then he had a drink from the intestine. There was enough water to keep him going for two days. When it was finished the nuns and the children would be safe and he would have to figure out what he did next. He stretched back against the rocks and continued to think about the woman who had named herself St Agnes.

The night before, when he and the old nun had sat staring up at the wondrous blanket of stars that seemed to be within reach of their hands, he had asked her what she thought about him. He remembered she had not responded right away. When she had finally spoken, her voice had a distant sound to it. He could hear her words as plainly as if she were sitting beside him now. 'God came to this canyon, Mr Swanson. He came and He touched us all. He sent you to us. And perhaps . . . just perhaps . . . you are not who you think you are.' She had been grinning at him when she said this last thing and he had responded sharply.

'Hokum,' he had said. 'I'm just me.'

She hadn't responded.

A while later he looked over at the pyramid of small stones. Even through the web of pain in his body, he felt better. Perhaps the best he'd felt in a long time. He wondered why. He'd been stung, shot, had an arm broke clean in two, nearly died of thirst, had his face fried like a buffalo steak and he felt okay. He laughed out loud. He pulled the Hawken close beside him and let his pistol rest in his lap. Things could be worse.

Locan tried to show no emotion as the warrior, Ponce, spoke. The old shaman was sitting next to him and he could feel his ancient body wincing as if the words were lashes. Jaco was also listening to the man and he seemed worried.

When the man had finished speaking, it was the shaman who spoke first.

'Our arrows strike him . . . our war clubs strike him . . . but still this white warrior lives. Can you continue to believe that we will triumph over him?'

The old man had stood up and his thin legs were trembling under him. He had stopped talking and was looking down at the sand. He suddenly realized that he had almost crossed over that thin line that separated the power of the shaman – power derived from the Other World – and the very real power of an Apache war leader. A shaman could advise, could argue, could plead . . . and the old man could certainly do this and more with Locan because of their many years together, but there was a faint line of respect that no shaman dared cross, and Cadette could feel that he was perilously close to it. Slowly, he raised his eyes and looked into Locan's huge face. The man was smiling good naturedly.

'Old man, I'm glad to see you still have passion. It is too bad there are no women in your wickiup to benefit from it.'

'Cadette makes a point.' It was Jaco's voice. The words were tentative and unsure. He knew that while Locan might laugh at a challenge from Cadette, he would not tolerate any form of insolence from him.

'What point?'

Jaco and the warrior, Ponce, exchanged nervous glances. Jaco understood that since he had made the comment he would have to answer Locan or face a shaming that he knew his leaf-thin reputation could not withstand. At the same time, he knew Locan would try and bait him into a fight. If this happened, Jaco knew he would die.

'Only that the man seems impossible for us to kill.'

'Are you afraid, Jaco?' The words were an insult.

'No more than Cadette or Ponce or any of my brothers. I think it is unwise for a man not to listen to a shaman.'

He was close to the edge, but he had been smart. He had chosen his words instinctively well, he had sided with his people, with the heritage and blood of the Apache, and now Locan was the one standing on the outside of the invisible ring, the one who had to be careful.

He rose quickly to his feet in one tremendous burst of energy and the others stepped back as if shoved. He was looking at Ponce with a pleasant expression on his face.

'I agree,' he said to Ponce. 'A man would be a fool to not follow the wise council of a shaman with the powers of Cadette. You agree, Ponce, my brother?' The words were not threatening and Ponce nodded.

'Then we all agree. And I, Locan, have done just that. I have listened to the wise words of Cadette. Listened when he told me that the vision I had only a short time ago was truly a vision from the People of the Dreams . . . a vision from the Other World.' He turned and looked at the old man. 'Did you not say this, Cadette?'

The old man nodded and wrapped the blanket he had been sitting on around his shoulders as if he were trying to keep out a biting cold.

Locan took a deep breath and pulled himself up to his full height. 'Of course the white warrior cannot be killed by our arrows and war clubs. He is one with the black robes and he shares their magic. Cadette has said this, and I believe it. But, – he paused and let the focus of his gaze move steadily to each man's face – 'but ... the People of the Dreams have given me the sign. We are not to try to kill the man. The spirits of the mountains wish to do it themselves. The white warrior will die from no water. All we must do is keep him penned up like a goat with the women and children in the enclosure.' His voice was rising, and now he was staring directly at Jaco. 'Surely this should not be difficult for Apache warriors. Should it, Jaco?'

The smaller man had dropped his stare. He shook his head.

Locan smiled a smile that was frightening to look at in its raw wildness. 'No, it should not ... not if those warriors do as their leader has asked and stay in the rocks of the river bed.'

Swanson had built a fire to cook some of the few remaining beans. Not because he wanted the beans, but because he wanted the Indians to know he was doing it. And if they happened to get off a lucky shot, then he wouldn't have to do any more figuring. Maybe his guardian angel would protect him. He grinned to himself. It was beginning to feel more like the old days. He guessed because he didn't have a bunch of kids and three nuns counting on him ... hanging on his every move. He checked his watch. The women had been on the trail for three hours. That would put them halfway down the mountain. Three more hours and they would be out into the desert and nearly safe from pursuit. Two hours after that, they would be at the water hole and a good forty miles ahead of the Apaches.

The Apaches could read sign as well as any man alive, and in the morning when they found the wagon's tracks they would read those tracks and know they were cold and wouldn't waste their time pursuing the nuns and the children. Especially if they knew someone was still trapped at the wagons. He stood and picked up the shovel again and banged on the wheel of the wagon once more.

He let his thoughts drift to the old nun. She was probably singing like a mountain canary now to that bunch of waifs. He was certain she had got over her anger. He didn't like to think of her mad. He let his thoughts return to her smile, the way it wrinkled the corners of her eyes and cut deep lines on her face. He thought of her lucky streak. She indeed led a charmed life ... maybe that's what happened when a woman took the veil.

He was glad she was safely away. After all, she was the reason he had come here in the first place. He felt tired and moved to the rocks and sat down. He drifted off.

Swanson couldn't believe his eyes when he awoke. He had to be dreaming. He shut his eyes and opened them again. The nagging pains in his body told him it was no dream. Sister St Agnes was sitting in the sand a few feet in front of him, staring at his face, smiling that smile of hers that exposed her two front teeth. He was too surprised to talk for a few seconds.

'What are you doing here? Did Sister Elizabeth lose control of the team?'

'You worry too much,' the old nun said. 'Everyone's fine.'

'Then why are you here?'

'Because I've never before met anyone sent by God.'

'Let's not joke. I risk my—'

'I'm not joking,' the old woman interrupted, standing and brushing her hands together. 'I'm quite serious. You were sent by God to save the children.'

'I was not. Say I saved the children if you want, but that's all.'

'Oh no,' she said, shaking her head. 'I prayed for you – or someone like you to be sent – and that same day you arrived.'

'Chance.'

'That was not chance. How many men would have looked at what was happening in this canyon, seen death waiting to strike us, as you did, and then would have voluntarily ridden into it? Very few, Mr Swanson. And of those who might have had the courage to sacrifice themselves, how many would have stumbled on this lonely place on the very same day I so desperately needed them, the very day I had prayed to God to send someone to save the children? No, not chance, Mr Swanson. You were sent by God. You must understand that.'

He watched her face for a long time before he spoke. All the feeling of relief that had flooded over him before had vanished.

'Why is this so important to you?'

'Because it is the most important thing that will ever happen in your life. Just as it's the most important thing that has ever happened in mine.' She was standing over him now. 'Mr Swanson, you have been touched by God.'

Swanson had heard her say that before. He started to raise his eyebrows, and then something in her face, the way her eyes pleaded with him, kept him from doing it.

'And that's why you came back?'

She studied his face. 'Yes, because I want you to know that you were sent by God . . . but also because I cannot let you die here alone.'

He took a drink of water from the intestine. 'If God bothered to send me to save the children – and I did – then why would He let me die here? That doesn't sound like a very fair God.'

'It's not our place to judge God.'

'No. You're not going to get off that easy. You tell me that I was sent here by God to rescue the children. And now you tell me that after I went ahead and mucked up my life to do what God asked me to do, I'm going to die here? And you think because you come down here to die with me that that makes it okay . . . evens the score kinda, right? Or did God send you here to die with me?'

'I don't know.'

'Why not? If you're so certain that I was sent here, why don't you know if you were sent here?'

'Because it doesn't work that way, Mr Swanson. Believe me.'

'Why should I believe someone who isn't certain of anything?'

'I don't know. I guess maybe you shouldn't.' She was staring at her hands. She moved away from him a few feet and settled herself back down on the sand.

'I want you to know something else,' she said, her voice low. She continued to stare at her hands as though they didn't belong to her. 'You saved my faith.'

'What's that supposed to mean? Ever since I got here you've been telling me how I was a messenger from God . . . how fortunate I was . . . and how I needed to have faith, and now you tell me that I saved your faith. I don't get it.'

'You should.'

'Why?'

'Because you yourself have given up and then recovered. I saw it when you were struggling up the hillside with the Apaches chasing you. I saw it in your face. You had quit, Mr Swanson. You had given up faith in yourself. Whatever belief you had in your own strength, you had lost it there on that hillside.' She looked across at him. 'You also gave up when the dog died. And it almost cost the children their lives. But you came back. Well, I did the same.'

He stared at the ground between them without saying anything. Then he looked back up at her and said, 'Why did you lose your faith?'

'I don't know, really. There was no one big reason. It just sort of wore down. I came to get the children because I have always loved children . . . not because I had great faith. After I returned, I had planned to leave the convent. And then when I realized I couldn't save the children myself, I did the only thing I knew how to do . . . I prayed to God for help. And He sent me you. And I knew again that He existed. That everything is all right under His heaven.' She was smiling her big two-tooth smile again. 'And, I can assure you, Mr Swanson, that's a wonderful feeling. I so wish you could feel it.'

He studied her face for a long time and then half smiled and said, 'Well, if everything is all right under heaven, then perhaps things aren't so bad after all.'

'I guarantee it.'

They didn't talk for a long time after that. Swanson sat against the rocks with the Hawken leaning next to him, feeling like he was lost and wandering in circles. The old nun was propped against a wall of sandstone mending a tear in her habit. Every few minutes she would look up at him and smile. He did not return the smiles. He was trying to force his mind to deal with the problem she had caused by returning. Without her, he could have taken his chances. He might even have been able to evade the Apaches and gotten out, though he doubted it. But now he had to worry about her, and he realized that death only seemed to hold some sort of power over him when he had others to worry about. Alone, he didn't think much about death . . . he had lived with it around enough to feel comfortable in its presence. But when he thought about the death of the old nun, it became something real and somehow more important than he knew it actually was.

When she was finished mending her habit, Sister St Agnes picked up her travelling bag and came and sat next to him.

'You play cards, Mr Swanson?'

The question surprised him. He watched as she searched through the contents of her bag.

'Well?' she said, still searching.

'I do.'

'Good.' She sat up straight, holding a worn deck of playing cards and a third of a bottle of Scotch.

'Well, I'll be —!'

Swanson watched her shuffle, then deal. Her hands moved the cards with a smoothness and familiarity bred of plenty of practice.

'You've played before,' he said, grinning.

'Three nights a week at the rectory.'

'Scotch there, too?'

'Mostly wine. But some Scotch. Why, do you think it's a sin to take a drink?'

'Never did myself.'

'Nor do I. Would you please get a fire going so we can see the cards?'

Swanson kindled a small fire and then took his pistol and limped out by the wagons and studied the darkness. He had a feeling the Indians were closer, but for a reason he couldn't explain they weren't trying any devilry. It was strange.

Before he turned back to join Sister St Agnes, he thought he saw something move far down the road. But when he studied it, he couldn't be certain. Perhaps it was a raccoon. No Apache was going to leave himself exposed on an open road on a moonlit night. Not with a man with a Hawken in the neighbourhood.

'Mr Swanson. Are you stalling?'

He was still watching the dark spot. He glanced at the old nun and then back at the road. The shadow was gone. For a fleeting second, he had a sense that something else equally surprising would happen this night.

They played poker. Five card, seven card, stud, draw. They played bucking horse, a game he knew. They played widow's walk, a game of hers. Thread the needle. Twister. They played for red beans. They drank Scotch. They argued. They laughed. They got tired of poker and she taught him gin rummy. They played it for beans as well. And when the Scotch was gone, she had all the beans; the last of them won on a wild bet of his.

He leaned back on his rolled-up blanket. 'I think you won fair.'

'You know I did.' She smiled and put her cards away.

'Guess I should keep my ranch then.'

'Absolutely.'

They both laughed hard and then sat quietly for a few minutes. She was looking out towards the canyon, while he watched the stars overhead.

'You know. You remind me of my mother.'

'I thought you didn't know her.'

'I didn't really. I was too young.' He continued to stare up at the dark sky. 'Maybe what I mean is, I'd like you to remind me of her. That make sense?'

'It does. And I'd be proud to remind you of her.'

'I wonder sometimes what she was like.'

'That isn't too hard to figure.'

Swanson stared at the old woman's face. 'It isn't?'

'No. Not at all.'

'Tell me then.' His voice had a wistful edge to it.

'Well, we know she had beautiful dark black hair. Thick and with a wave.'

'How can you know something like that?'

'Hair passes from mother to son, Mr Swanson. Believe me. Your mother had the hair I described. And her skin was very fair, her features fine and beautiful. I imagine she had your fine bone structure. Yes, I'm sure of it.'

Swanson was staring at the stars again. 'Was she tall?'

'Yes, she was a tall woman with a wonderfully graceful build, soft yet strong. But that wasn't the best of her beauty. Her real beauty came in her person. She was quiet and gentle. But she could stand up if need came a-knocking. She liked to laugh and she liked other people. And she believed in them.'

The old nun gazed at him. Tears were running down his cheeks. He closed his eyes. She stood and picked up her travelling bag and looked down at him and smiled.

'And you know what, Mr Swanson? Your mother loved

her children more than anything else in the world. She loved you deeply, Mr Swanson. She still loves you deeply. Of that, I can guarantee you. You may not have known it, but you've been loved every day of your life by God and your mother. No mother stops loving her child just because she's gone. Love isn't killed that easily.'

Swanson dreamed the second dream of his life this night. It was of his mother. And this time he knew what she looked like and how she moved and spoke. It was the most wonderful moment he had ever felt in his life. And when he finally, reluctantly, awoke, the second surprise he had expected was there in the enclosure.

The boy Matthew was sitting in the sand staring out at the canyon. Swanson went and sat down next to him and handed him the water bag.

'Matt, what happened? Are the others okay?'

Although it was almost imperceptible, he thought the boy nodded his head. He was sweating and filthy from crawling through the brush.

Swanson sat there watching him drink and feeling a strange change taking place inside him. He felt as trapped as ever. Only this time, he didn't feel so alone. His mother loved him . . . the old nun had come back for him. Swanson went to the small pyramid of stones and dug his deed out. Maybe things weren't done yet. There might yet be a way out of here after all. For whatever reason, the Apaches didn't want to attack them. He would sleep and study on it in the morning.

Day Five...

_____

The two young Apaches were scared. It was not visible on their faces, but fear gripped them like a hand deep in their bowels, tightened over their muscles and pounded in their blood. Horses and mules had been stolen from them. Worse, the horses and mules had been used by the black robes and the white warrior. They had finished telling what they knew to their leader more than an hour before and he had not yet spoken to them. Instead, he had sent others to confirm what they had told him. And now four of them, Locan, the shaman Cadette, and the two of them, waited in front of the wickiup. None of them spoke. The ancient one was sitting and working his bony fingers over a beaded amulet. Every so often his lips moved silently. Locan sat opposite him, cross-legged, determinedly honing the blade of his knife against a stone. The blade shone like silver, and though the knife was over twelve inches long it looked small in the Apache's giant hand. It was bladed on both sides. A knife for killing. Hunched over in this manner, his huge shoulders and arms moving the blade in quick slicing motions over the stone with a *chrrrring* sound sent chills racing over the skin of the young men.

Locan did not look up from his task when Ponce, Jaco and three other warriors trotted up to them. The men were breathing hard. Deep in their eyes there was a drawn look of concern. No one spoke until the old shaman nodded at Ponce. The warrior glanced at the top of Locan's head to see if he was going to look up. He looked back worriedly at the old shaman, who nodded again.

'The wagon at the spring and four of the animals are gone. There are tracks from the enclosure up the far trail of the canyon, to the rim. They loaded the wagon there and took it down the main trail out of the mountains. They have been gone for all of the night. They must be far out in the desert now, past the watering place, on the main road to the fort.' He paused and caught a breath that he didn't really need. Locan was still whetting the knife against the stone, and the sound it made caused them all to tense.

'If we pursued them' – he hesitated, glancing nervously at Jaco and the other men – 'we would not reach them before they arrived at the hacienda of the whites that sits against the far mountains. Those that left in the wagon are safe.'

The words seemed to splash from Ponce's mouth on to them like mud. No one spoke. Locan continued to hone the two edges of the knife. The only sound was of steel against rock – a death song sung by a tool of man to cold stone.

'And you say that the white warrior and at least one of the black robes remain? Is that right?' Cadette spoke quietly to control the surges of fear and anger that rushed through his old body.

None of the warriors answered.

'Jaco, is that right?'

The warrior jumped. He had tried to stay out of it, tried to let Ponce do the talking. And, now, here was the stupid old man asking him to answer. He began to shake and he gripped the war club in his hand harder to hide his fear. He had to do something. If he didn't, Locan would kill him.

'That is right, Cadette. The white warrior is still ours. As is the old black robe. Negra says that is the one. She is the one of the most power.' So far, it was going all right. But he couldn't be certain. Locan still had not spoken. He felt panic rising in his stomach as he watched the large Indian sitting on the ground as if deaf. He felt the urge to raise his war club and to smash it down on Locan's skull. Then they would find out how strong he was. He would die like other men. Snapping at the dirt. But Jaco knew he would never do it. He had a catlike quickness, but not the courage to do it. And even if he had, he did not want to face a life of banishment. He had to survive some other way.

'Yes, we still have the warrior and the old one. But . . . we should have them all,' Jaco said. He was looking at the two young boys. They could be no more than fourteen summers. They avoided his eyes and stared off into the hills. That they were scared was obvious. But they were Apache and masked their fear well. 'The horses were stolen from under our noses. Men we had trusted did not keep the trust. They must be punished.'

When Jaco stopped talking, the only sound was the boys' breathing, each breath sounding as if it might be their last. Then Locan laughed. He did not lift his head, he did not stop grinding the knife, he simply laughed. All eyes were locked on him.

'You say that Negra says the old one remains with the white warrior?' Locan's voice was low and steady.

'That is right.'

'You have not seen her for yourself?'

'No. I believe Negra.'

'I believe a brave man, too. It is a coward I do not believe.' Suddenly, he stopped moving the blade of the knife and looked up at Jaco. He was squinting into the sun and could only see the dark outline of the smaller man. Jaco was cunning and could strike like a rattlesnake. The sun would blind the large Indian for a split second if he came at him. Locan continued to stare boldly into the glare, focusing on the dark shape standing before him.

'And you, Jaco, are a coward. You would blame boys for your mistakes. You are like a slinking coyote that haunts the fringes of the camp, stealing scraps of everything ... food, women, courage ... scaring the little children ... howling bravely to the moon until a dog spots you and runs you off and you are seen for what you are. A coward.'

Jaco could see that Locan had the knife by its leather handle in an underhand grip. Slowly, he shortened up on the rawhide wrapping of the club. He stepped back a few inches, judging the distance carefully.

'Other men sleep with your woman and still you do nothing.'

His heart was banging wildly in his chest and Locan's words were almost unintelligible to him now. Jaco's eyes leaped quickly from face to face. No one would help him. He stepped back a few more inches. He fought the urge to flee.

'I told you to move the men into the rocks of the river.

To pen the white warrior up like a goat so that he could not escape. But you did not do this. You hid by the campfires, afraid of the dark. It is you who must be punished.'

Jaco had completed the sentence in his mind before Locan spoke the words, and as the huge man started to rise Jaco's war club was already in its vicious descending arc. Jaco had seen Locan fight many times and he had always watched in awe at the speed and reflexes of the giant man. Even so, he was surprised by the quick jerk of Locan's head that caused the club to strike him only a glancing blow to the side of his skull before burying itself with a sickening thunk in the fleshy part of his shoulder.

Jaco leaped away and grabbed a short lance from one of the warriors standing in a gathering crowd. He whirled and faced Locan. Locan was on his feet now, one half of his body drenched in blood, an ear hanging by a thin piece of skin, the war club still sticking in his shoulder. He looked dazed from the blow. He wavered unsteadily on his large legs. Jaco's courage surged. He would do it. He would finish Locan while he stood there stupidly tasting his own blood. He would drive the lance through his stomach and pin him to the ground and let him die slowly, screaming to be killed. He studied the man's face to be certain. The eyes were far away, glazed. No man could fake that look. He gripped the shaft in both his hands with all his might and lunged forward.

Locan seemed to pull himself in tighter, to compress his large body as the smaller, quicker man rushed him, but he was too dazed to leap to the side. He swiped clumsily with his free hand at the blade of the lance as it sped towards his middle, knocking it off its deadly trajectory. Still, it wasn't enough and the blade cut into the flesh above his hip and plunged through with a popping sound until Jaco's hand hit him in the stomach. With surging confidence, the little warrior tried to back up and pull the lance free. Then he saw a flash of bright light in his eyes, and felt a faint scratch and thought at first that Locan had caught him with a fingernail. He started to laugh. Then he heard a deep gurgling sound and realized that his throat had been cut. He fell forward on his hands and knees and gnawed and spit and bit at his tongue until it was almost off.

Locan kicked the dying man in the side so hard that the sound of breaking ribs could be heard above the rasping noise of Jaco's open windpipe. He turned and stared blindly at the gathering of warriors. No one moved. No one spoke. With deliberation, Locan reached out a hand and yanked the war club out of his shoulder, turning as he did and burying the blade deep into Jaco's back. The small man quivered and then was still. Locan grasped the lance sticking through his side and tried to yank it out, but could not.

'Ponce,' he screamed.

The man stepped forward.

'Pull it free.'

When the lance was out, Locan stood waiting for his head to clear. Cadette approached him cautiously, stopping a few feet in front of him. Covered with blood, Locan looked frightening. No one moved in the crowd.

'And what do you say, Cadette?'

'I say you killed to defend your life. But I also say that it is over here. That the spirits are against us in this place. You are a brave and a wise man, Locan, but you cannot stop the black robes and the white warrior. We must leave.'

'No,' Locan said, wobbly on his legs. He took a step and then sat down hard. 'No. We will not leave. Before the setting of the sun tomorrow, I will climb to the wagons and destroy the white man and the black robe.'

A fearful murmur rose from the warriors who watched. Cadette, too, looked frightened.

'Your sign was water. You yourself told us that the mountain spirits wanted to destroy the white man. That he would die of thirst. That we were not to kill him ourselves.' The old man paused and studied the face of Locan. He could find no expression.

Slowly, Locan turned and looked up at the old man. 'And you, Cadette, said you could not be certain that this was true. So I will wait no longer. I will kill him. Before tomorrow's sun has disappeared over the ridge of the west canyon wall, I will destroy him.' His eyes moved aggressively over the faces of the men. 'If there is any man here who would oppose me, let him speak now.' No one moved.

'I want every man down in the rocks below the wagon. I will go with you to prove that neither the white man nor the black robe is to be feared. And tomorrow you will watch me rise from the rocks of the river bed and destroy them both.'

It was the very first of morning on the fifth day. Swanson was almost too stiff to stand. But he was happy. As happy as he had ever recalled being. The boy was curled up in the sand asleep a few feet in front of him. Sister St Agnes was cooking breakfast over a small fire at the far side of the enclosure. Swanson pulled his pistol and checked its cylinder. Then he hobbled to the wagons and took his telescope from his pack. He slid the silvery tube out until it was almost as long as his arm and had a look. For a brief moment, he saw a quick movement of colour in the rocks of the dry river bed and then all was still. He panned the lens over the chaparral of the mountains and the rim of the canyon. He saw nothing else. But he knew what the colour meant. He stretched and then casually walked over and picked up the Hawken where it leaned against the rocks and strolled back to the wagons. He stood idly watching the canyon with the heavy rifle cradled in the crook of his broken arm. Sister St Agnes glanced at him once or twice but continued to cook. The boy slept. The day was going to be as hot as the ones before, stretching seemingly endlessly out into burning days of sand, wind, mirages and rocks.

Swanson let his eyes wander back to where the corpse of Sister Ruth sat staring up at him. The scavengers had been at the body for three nights, and the flesh of both legs were stripped off to bone. The sun had parched the eyeless face until it had the look of a dried apple; a shrivelled, hideous smile lay frozen over the features. Fortunately, the heat and sun had desiccated the flesh to the point where it no longer stank. Swanson studied it a moment longer and then threw the rifle to his shoulder and fired.

The explosion of powder created a concussion of air that smashed into the far wall of the canyon and then rebounded on to the cliffs behind Swanson. Sister St Agnes stood up straight as if slapped by the sound. The boy was struggling to sit up.

Swanson had fired at an exposed boot. It was gone now. He didn't know if he'd hit anything. It didn't matter.

The shot would keep them cautious and far enough away from the wagons. He smelled the last of the venison frying and walked over to the fire.

Sister St Agnes watched him as he approached.

'You're going to burn that if you're not careful.'

'Why must you persist in trying to kill people?'

'I'm not, ma'am. I'm trying to keep us alive.'

'I'm certain God will provide.' She turned and knelt down at the skillet.

Swanson watched her thin back and the black cloth that flowed off the back of her head. He was feeling better and in a mood to tease her.

'How can you say that?'

'What?'

'That God will provide. You told me last night that God was going to repay me for saving the children by letting me die in this – I guess it's fair to say – godforsaken canyon.' He was grinning.

She did not answer him or look up. She continued to poke at the frying strips of meat with a fork. Swanson waited for her to respond. She did not.

Uncomfortable, he turned and walked to a point where he was out from under the overhang of the mountain and stared up at the rugged rock face rising hundreds of feet above him. It was steep and dangerous looking. He glanced back at the old nun. She seemed small and worn out, hunched as she was over the fire. The boy had come and sat beside her, and she handed him a plate of steaming meat. He ate it eagerly, quickly, as the grease burned his fingers.

'Only trying to make a joke.'

'It's not the kind of joke I'll join you in.' Her voice was firm, but not angry.

'No harm meant.'

'Fine. Would you like some breakfast?'

'Sure,' he said, squatting down next to Matthew. He looked at the boy's sleepy eyes. 'How you doing, son?'

The boy didn't respond to the question. Swanson watched him for a second and then turned to Sister St Agnes.

'You suppose he understands me?'

The old nun ran her fingers through the boy's hair, trying to smooth it out.

'Matthew is as smart as anybody. He's just quiet, that's all.' She smiled warmly at the boy. 'I like that in a man.'

When they were done eating, Swanson rolled a smoke and lit it in the flames of the campfire.

'I didn't know you smoked.'

'Sometimes.'

'Do you have the makings for another?'

Nat's eyebrows rose over his smile. 'Sister, you never fail to amaze me. Want me to roll it?'

'I'll roll my own.'

They sat enjoying the morning and smoking. The boy was sitting quietly next to the old nun. Swanson moved his good arm quickly and snatched an earless lizard off a rock. He pulled a small string out of his shirt pocket and tied a noose around its neck. The lizard turned its head and eyed him. He put it on the dark shirt the boy was wearing and let its skin turn a dark, dusky green. Then he picked it up and set it down on the white sand. The boy watched. In a few minutes, the lizard was so white that he was difficult to see against the sand. The boy watched it, but he didn't move. Finally, Swanson picked the lizard up and set him in Matthew's lap. He stood and walked to the wagons and watched the river. He motioned for Sister St Agnes to join him.

'They're in the river now.'

'I don't see them.'

'I can smell them.'

Sister St Agnes chuckled, then realized he was serious. 'I can't.'

'I can. It's the food they eat . . . mule, mice, cactus.'

'You're not kidding?'

'Nope. They carry less scent than a white man, but what they carry is plain enough to smell. They're close now.'

She took air into her nostrils. 'I still don't smell anything. What's it like?'

'Like cooking hominy.'

She tried again and still couldn't get the scent and gave up. 'Will they rush us?'

'Not during the day. But they'll come tonight. They've finally lost their patience.'

'We could hide in the cave.'

'And be buried alive. No thanks.'

'What then?'

'I've got an idea.' He turned away and studied the river rocks. 'I want to think on it.'

It was mid-afternoon when Swanson came and sat down next to Sister St Agnes. She was napping in the shade of the overhang. She stirred when he cleared his throat and then sat up. He handed her the intestine and she drank.

'We don't have many choices.'

She nodded and put the water down, catching her breath.

'If they're in the rocks of the river, can we still get out that way?' she asked.

'No. They're no more than a few yards down the slope. They've sealed us off pretty good. And they'll be expecting us to try that again. No, I think our only choice is to go over the mountain. They'll not expect it and we won't leave a trail.'

Her eyes widened. 'Over this mountain,' she said, putting a hand on the rock wall.

'The same.'

'Mr Swanson, that mountain must be five hundred feet straight up.'

Swanson stood and brushed his pants off. He looked at her and smiled. 'More like one thousand. Have a little faith, Sister.'

'Remember the old Testament line: "Do not tempt the Lord thy God."'

Swanson had chosen to leave the enclosure in the brilliant sun of the high afternoon. He knew it was the most difficult time for a man to see into the harsh rays of the noon sun, even harder than night when the pupils of the eyes opened wide to gather extra light from the moon and stars.

They had been climbing slowly for over two hours, and had moved two hundred feet up the hard, hostile mountainside. It was exhausting, dangerous work. Swanson stopped on the faint trail that stitched thinly over hard limestone. The old nun was struggling a few feet in front of him, bent over under the weight of the Hawken. He looked up at the mountain. It broke into three giant minarets of stone stabbing the sky like three thick fingers. Rough chaparral filled the canyons between the granite peaks. His eyes scanned the rocks. The peaks were towering white spikes, each faced with a maze of cliffs and broken terraces, burning and flooded with sunlight that exploded out of a vast, arching blue sky. It was breathtaking in both its beauty and its enormity. The thought of climbing higher seemed to numb him and he looked at Sister St Agnes. The old nun had reached the top of the large rock she was climbing and was looking back. He raised a finger as a signal to wait, then he began his own ascent up the side of the rock, carefully inserting his feet and hands into the small clefts that had been cut into the stone eons ago by what the Apaches called the Ancient Ones. The boy clung tightly to his back. The climbing was made all the more difficult by the wound in his leg and the broken arm. He was breathing hard when he reached the top, and he let the boy down and sat next to the old nun.

Sister St Agnes was staring out across the vast expanse of desert that spread as far as the eye could see. She was smiling.

'What's funny?'

'Not funny. Magnificent. The starkness and the simplicity are as beautiful as anything in God's creation. As I was climbing, Mr Swanson, I had the feeling nature was jealously guarding God's beloved work. Did you feel that?'

'Not exactly.'

Sister St Agnes ignored the remark. 'I feel like I've been here before.'

Swanson scratched his head. 'Maybe you have.'

'How do you mean?'

'The Indians believe a man comes back and lives his life

over again. Maybe you're doing that. Your people were here two hundred years ago.'

'My people?'

'Catholics. They were the first explorers here. The friars of the Franciscan Order up from Mexico. They came through here trying to get to California and every time they got lost they said it was God's punishment for their sins.' He laughed. 'They left a bunch of saints' names like yours scattered all over the place. They surely must have sinned.'

The old nun sat thinking for a few minutes and then gazed off across the land and asked, 'Rain?'

Swanson glanced at the white cumulus clouds which had begun to mass in enormous bunches in the north. They were stately, immutable as sculptured stone, dead white against the massive blue vault of sky.

'False promises. We've got a lot of creeks and clouds but no water.'

'That's too bad,' she said wistfully.

Swanson watched the side of her face as he passed the boy the intestine of water. 'You like this place, don't you?'

'I love it. It's as beautiful as the great cathedrals of Europe. It's so grand it renews your soul.' She turned and looked at him. 'You?'

'It's a good enough land, I guess. Kind of inhospitable. Kill a man who doesn't know it. But that's not the worst. The worst is even if you know it, it's a meagre living. California's the place. Grow your own fruit. Eat grapes evenings on your own front porch and watch your cattle fattening on green grass.'

'What else matters to you, Mr Swanson?'

He continued to let his eyes drift over the miles of desert. 'I don't know.'

'I think very few things. But those things matter very much.'

Swanson stood up too quickly and the pain shot through his leg. He bent and let the boy crawl on to his back. 'We better climb higher. I'll lead. I have a feeling about this place.'

'What feeling?'

'That it's been used before for what we want to use it for now.'

Sister St Agnes didn't quite understand.

When the main trail in the rocks veered left, Swanson turned to the right and followed the bare rocks that led around a huge sandstone tower. The trail became blind for a distance. There were no hand-holds, no worn footpaths in the stone. It was barren and windswept here. They crawled slowly along. Swanson's eyes searched through the cliffs and the ragged rocks as they struggled forward. To the unskilled eye, they had lost the trail completely and were climbing over trackless, perilous wastes of shale and sandstone, moving fruitlessly over treacherous terraces and up blind passages. But to Swanson's practised gaze, they were simply unravelling the intentionally misleading wanderings of ancient minds who had used these same mountains for refuge. From whom or what, he did not know.

At a narrowing place in the trail, Swanson carefully led the old nun past an ancient deadfall made of large rocks. The trap's trigger was a small collection of stones laid masterfully across the trail. The stones were so thinly balanced that Swanson figured a gentle brush from a moccasin would send a river of deadly rock crashing down on its victims.

Later, as they were moving over a slope of granite, he stopped and stood looking at a large pillar of stone that rose straight up some three hundred feet from the canyon floor. He sensed the feeling again. He was close. The pillar was connected to the slope of granite on one side. A small ledge of stone, no more than six inches wide, traced a ribbon around the rock to whatever it was that was on the other side. Swanson sat down and studied the pillar and the small ledge for a few minutes. The pillar was a good thirty feet in diameter. The ledge seemed frail but intact. Swanson dug into his pack and pulled out a rawhide rope that he had taken from the wagons. He secured one end around a large rock and tied the other end around his waist. Sister St Agnes watched him. The boy squatted, looking out at the desert.

Swanson stood and stretched his sore muscles. 'You and the boy wait here.'

Sister St Agnes looked at the ledge and then back at him. 'I'm not certain it'll hold you. I'm lighter.'

'Thanks. But it's my rope.'

Swanson faced the stone and carefully put a foot out on the ledge. His heart was beating hard. He pushed down, slowly transferring his weight from the larger piece of granite where the nun and the boy sat watching him on to the narrow strip. It held. He inched forward. Now both his feet were on the ledge. He was committed. If it gave way under him, he would pitch into space, falling and praying that the rawhide rope would hold him. His arms were spread wide, wet palms against the stone as if he were trying to hug it. Sweat ran into his eyes and his breath came in short jerks. The tension mounted as he moved out farther on the ledge. Then he felt it and knew that his hunch had been right. It was a small handhold. Then another. And another. Others had gone before him. It was not long before he had inched his way round the pillar. He stepped out on to a flat skillet of black rock. His clothes were drenched in sweat. The place where he stood was circular in shape and fifty feet across. At the far end there was a shallow cave cut into the hillside. Swanson could hear water. Quickly, he untied the rope from his waist and crossed over to the sound. It was dripping steadily down a long finger of stone from a hidden spring, dripping into a large rock cistern. Eagerly, he plunged his face in it and drank the icy fluid until he thought he would burst. When his thirst had slackened somewhat and when he couldn't hold any more water, he heard the old nun calling his name softly from around the rocks. He moved back to the point where the pillar and the rock ledge began. The curve in the stone prevented him from seeing her or the boy.

'Sister?'

'Yes?' came the reply.

'I'm on the other side.'

'I always knew you would make it,' she teased.

'The other side of the pillar. There's water, a cave. I'll be back in a few minutes.'

He turned back to the cave. Something in it drew him. It was tall enough to stand in and some fifteen feet wide at its face. It was shallow, maybe twenty feet deep, and filled with clean sand. The rear of the cave was thick with shadows and, after the bright light of the mountains, Swanson was sun blinded. A circle of blackened rocks and ashes indicated that the cave had been inhabited at an earlier time. But that time had been long ago.

Swanson saw some baskets and a small piece of pottery sitting against the wall. These were filled with dried maize, acorns and berries. There was a tattered piece of woven mat that had disintegrated with age. The pottery shard was decorated with little figures of men, birds and beasts in red. He had never seen a design like this one. It wasn't Apache or Comanche. Then his eye caught on her face in the thinning shadows and he was filled with a strange sense of awe.

He stood up slowly. At the back of the cave, laid out on a stone ledge, was the almost perfectly preserved mummy of a young Indian woman, her skin still whole, her teeth perfect, her hair tied down with beads of quartz and turquoise. Her hands were folded tenderly over her chest. She was completely naked except for a leather breech-cloth. And crouched next to her, leaning as if asleep against the ledge, lay the mummy of a young man. Swanson stood staring for a long time. What had happened in this place? What mystery? Had these been lovers? How long had they lain here? Had the girl died of natural causes and had the young man in his grief chosen suicide? Or had a father or a husband found them in a forbidden tryst and killed them both? Sister St Agnes' voice brought Swanson out of his thoughts and out of the cave. He went to the edge of the chasm and called to her softly.

'I'd given you up for lost,' she returned.

'I tied the rawhide on a rock on the other side. I want you to go over the way I did, facing the wall, palms out. Don't look down at your feet. Stare straight ahead at the wall. And don't reach for the rope. It'll exert pressure on your back, but don't lean into it whatever you do. Can you do it?'

Sister St Agnes nodded at his instructions, and moved briskly into position. She took a deep breath and mumbled a small prayer, then she started across. The old nun made the dangerous passage without difficulty or seemingly any real concern. She was a marvel, he thought. Swanson brought the boy over on his back.

The three of them stood quietly in the shadows of the cave, staring at the mummified remains of the young brave and the Indian maiden. Matthew seemed as touched by the scene as was the old nun or Swanson. The light was weak and melancholy-feeling, and catheral-like where the bodies lay.

'Sad,' Swanson said softly.

'No,' Sister St Agnes replied. 'Wonderful. Man's love and devotion to man. It's a pure gift from God. These two obviously possessed it.' She crossed herself and knelt beside them.

After St Agnes had prayed over them, Swanson hung a blanket between the bodies and the rest of the cave. He and the old nun had agreed they should not disturb the couple's eternal rest. The man and woman were at peace now no matter how tragic had been the circumstance of their death. Swanson and Sister St Agnes wanted to leave them that way.

The boy sat squatting at the far edge of the ledge, staring out across the desert that sprawled in a vast tract of land to where the sun was sinking. Swanson walked over to join him. He stopped with a start and crouched down.

'Matt, come back here.'

The boy did as he was told. Swanson crawled forward

and peered down over the edge of the rock. Their stone perch was located directly over the dry river bed and a few yards to the left of the wagons. And while they were two hundred feet up into the mountain, an Apache looking their way would catch movement or colour in the rocks. Swanson backed up and then in a half crouch went and pulled his telescope from his pack. He returned to the edge and lay down, panning the desert below. He counted ten Indians hiding in the rocks of the dry river bed. They were watching the wagons intensely. They hadn't spotted the boy. He slid away and sat next to him.

'Indians down there. Best stay away.' The boy didn't look at him or respond.

Swanson helped Sister St Agnes prepare a small fire of dried mesquite root that they had found in the cave. It was smokeless and there was enough sunlight left in the late afternoon sky that the flames would not be seen.

The meal was boiled beans, rice and small cakes of baked acorn meal that Swanson had made. Sister St Agnes had tried the acorns in the baskets. The dry desert air had preserved them but when she shelled one and ate it the meat had a sharp, bitter taste that stayed with her even after she had rinsed her mouth a couple of times. Swanson took the basket of acorns from her and picked up a small stone mortar and pestle that lay in the corner of the cave. After he had washed the dust from these ancient tools and rinsed the acorns, he showed the boy how to crack off the outer shell to get at the meat.

The boy worked steadily and carefully. When the pile of shelled acorns made a handful, Swanson put them into the pestle and began to grind them into flour. The boy continued to shell. Swanson sifted the fine powder out and left the coarser grains to be reground. When they were done, Swanson took a clean cloth from his pack that he kept for dressing wounds and put the flour in it, catching up the sides until he held the flour in a large cloth ball. He filled a pot with fresh water from the spring and then held the flour in it, swishing it around for a good half hour, washing the tannic acid out of it. When the water was the colour of weak tea, Swanson took fresh water and began to mix it with the damp flour, kneading it until he had a thick dough. He shaped this into small cakes and wrapped them in husks he found in the basket of maize and baked these in the ashes of the fire. They were tasty and filling.

After dinner, he and Sister St Agnes sat against the lava rocks of the mountain sharing Swanson's last cigarette and staring out at the fading tapestry of the desert. The boy sat close to the old nun, opening and shutting the blade of the pocket knife. A small white-winged dove landed on the flat stone of the ledge a few feet away from them and began to softly call for its mate: "Who-cooks-for-you?" . . . Who-cooks-for-you?"

'They must have been very happy here.'

He nodded.

'How long ago did they die?'

'I'd say seventy-five years ago, but maybe as much as one hundred. It's hard to know for sure. The desert air dries things pretty fast and thoroughly so they stay preserved.'

'Yes. I read once that they have found seeds which were still good after having lain in the tombs of the Pharaohs for almost four thousand years.'

The afternoon shadows were beginning to crawl out of the rocks and spread in pools across the ledge. The day was still hot. Far off in the distance, in the gathering twilight that bunched between the sand and the deepening blue roof of sky, the mass of cumulus clouds bumped against a serrated range of mountains and sent bolts of lightening stitching brilliant streaks of light to the ground. They saw the flashes first, and Swanson was surprised. He counted seconds until he heard the deep roll of thunder.

'Thirty miles away.'

'Just so long as someone gets some.'

The thunderstorm was beautiful, wild and brief. When it was over, the sun had pushed its way down to the edge of the planet. It was the start of evening. The growing darkness seemed to etch the trail that snaked below them toward Santa Fe with dark ink. The moon was just up in the eastern sky. Swanson shivered under a chill wind that rose like a wave over the rocks. He was feeling good.

'Hello, Grandmother,' he said to the moon.

'Why do you call her that?'

'That's what the Indians call her.'

'And the stars?'

'The souls of cousins that protect mankind.'

'I like that.'

Swanson stretched his good arm above his head and started to stand. Then he saw him.

The giant Indian had somehow worked his way around the ledge without any of them seeing or hearing him. He was stripped to his breechcloth and buckskin teguas, and holding a long-barrelled Colt Walker .44 calibre revolver that looked almost toy-like in his huge hand, and he had been in a fight, his head, shoulders and waist wrapped in bloody bandages. Hatred leaped from his broad face and thin cut eyes. Swanson guessed his height at six and a half feet, and his weight at close to two hundred and sixty pounds. Swanson didn't move. He was unarmed. His pistol, the Hawken, the crossbow, even his knife, were all in the cave. He hadn't been this careless outside a town in years. He wanted to kick himself. Just when it had seemed they were so close. Out the corner of his eye he saw the boy open the pocket knife and grasp it by the blade. Locan's eyes were locked on Swanson's face, examining it square inch by square inch. There was no curiosity, just disdain and hate. The boy moved his arm back slowly. Swanson knew what he was going to do. He snaked an arm out across the old nun and grabbed the boy's arm before he could throw.

'No chance, boy. Give me the knife.'

The Indian had crouched and balanced the pistol in his hand as soon as Swanson moved. Swanson took the knife when the boy handed it to him, folded the blade and then tossed it out on the rock in front of them. The Indian waved the barrel of the pistol at Swanson, motioning him away from the old nun and the boy. Swanson stood and stepped over in front of the open edge of the rock. His heart was pounding hard against his chest cavity. Fragments of things ... the dog, his brother's face, Anna, his mother's voice jumped through his thoughts. The Indian had the barrel of the pistol pointed at his chest. Swanson felt a cold, clammy shivering chill steal over him.

'No,' Sister St Agnes yelled, standing and moving quickly between Swanson and the Indian.

'Get out of the way,' Swanson said.

'No. You can't die this way. Not now.'

The boy had struggled to his feet and he had wrapped his arms around the old nun's thin waist. The three of them stood facing the giant Indian.

Swanson wasn't certain when he first became aware of the faint humming sound in the evening air; it just seemed as if it had always been there inside his skull. He listened. It was building slowly. It was like the steady, drumming trot of some feral creature coming out of the high altitudes in the west. Coming fast. Slowly, the *humm* was changing into a distant noise, rushing relentlessly over the sands, surging through canyons and streambeds, consuming mile after mile of terrain. On and on it came, until it was rapidly growing into a thunderous roar – blasting and foaming and leaping – a massive wall of wild brown water, mud and trees ravaging everything in its path. It was still coming. Rushing hungrily towards them, deafening and frightful.

Stunned by its ferocity, Swanson was even more surprised by its impact on the giant Indian. The man's small eyes grew wide; his expression one of shock as the raging sound grew louder. He was no longer staring at Swanson; instead his eyes were fixed on Sister St Agnes. Her medicine was responsible for this; she had summoned the storm to save her. He looked dazed. Then he visibly shook himself, struggling for control of his emotions.

The man leaped to the edge of the rock ledge, the pistol no longer pointed at Swanson. What he saw made him physically shudder. He stood trembling and staring in disbelief as a huge wave of boiling water and mud suddenly exploded down the narrow canyon below, the noise shattering the evening. Swanson whirled and looked over the edge and saw the violence and pandemonium breaking loose.

Those Apaches who had been hiding in the streambed were trying desperately to scramble to higher ground to flee the fury of the oncoming waters. It was useless. The flood rushed forward faster than a horse could run – a twenty-foot wall of death. Men were screaming and running and dying. Some drowned, swept under the raging flood. Others were smashed by the large rocks rolling with the waters. One was impaled by a small tree that had been thrown like a javelin by the roaring tempest.

Then suddenly the silence returned. It was eerie and still. The raging water was gone. Only wet sand and rocks and scattered pools of it remained. Three or four Indians were weakly pulling themselves up the sides of the river. They looked half dead. The others had simply disappeared, swept away by the exploding torrent of violent water.

When Swanson turned back, the Indian was gone.

Day Six …

S wanson lay on the edge of the rock in the hot splash of
the morning sunlight watching the two of them. He
had been studying them through his telescope since dawn.
They stood so absolutely still they could have been dead.
Neither seemed to even breathe. They didn't twitch, shift
a foot, or scratch. They didn't talk. They just stared up at
the mountain ledge where Swanson lay. The big Indian
towered over the elfin one. The old man was wearing a
kilt and a funny headgear. Two war ponies stood behind
them. And something else, something that Swanson
couldn't quite figure, was lying on the ground in front of
them under a blanket.

When he had first seen them, the sun had just begun
shooting bursts of light over the edges of the canyon. Now,
it was near zenith . . . and they hadn't moved. They knew
he was watching them. They knew the Hawken could
reach out and kill in an instant, could send a ball of lead
smashing into them before the sound of the shot ever
reached the river. Still they stood there, motionless, blindly
staring up at him.

Sister St Agnes and the boy came and sat down close to
him. They didn't speak. The nun watched the Indians,

fascinated. The boy looked over their heads at the distant mountains. After a while, a longtailed kangaroo rat came out of the rocks and scurried close to where the boy sat. There was a piece of the acorn cake lying on the stones there and he stuffed it into his cheeks. Swanson shifted his weight to get comfortable and the little beast made a leap of some eight feet back into the sand between the boulders. Swanson jumped reflexively, then went back to watching the pair. The mountains were steeped in silence.

'What do you think?'

'I think it's over.'

'Meaning?'

'I don't understand it, but when the water killed those Apaches in the river, it nearly killed the big Indian as well.'

'Do you trust them?'

'I trust any man who has the drop on me with a .44 and lets me live.'

They stood facing each other, Swanson and the big Indian, both staring into the other's eyes, neither betraying their thoughts or speaking. From the moment they had seen the nun walk out of the mountains and over to where they stood by the river's edge, the two Indians had fought hard to control their emotions. The big one had grasped the corners of a beautiful red and white blanket and waved it over his head, then thrown it skyward and allowed it to fall to the earth. It was a sign of peace. Somewhere deep inside their beings they were badly frightened. Something awful had happened to them. They had been punished by their gods. They were scared. The big Indian's life as an Apache war chief had been destroyed. But Swanson had no way of knowing any of this. He knew only that they were beaten men. He'd seen men like this before after gun fights or battles. They were soundly beaten. Neither was armed. The leader waved his massive hand and arm in an expansive way at the mound under the blanket and uttered a word that Swanson didn't understand. From the gesture, he guessed it was another peace offering of some sort. Then both he and Sister St Agnes saw the red hair lying on top of the blanket.

'It's Sister Ruth,' the old nun said, moving towards the blanket and the Indians. The two Apaches fell back as if she carried a deadly disease. Sister St Agnes dropped to her knees with a sigh and put her hands tenderly on the blanket. Swanson looked at the big Indian. The man was staring down at the sister. Swanson chose not to press their advantage.

'We go,' he said, pointing off toward Santa Fe.

The big Indian looked at him.

'Santa Fe,' Swanson said, still pointing.

'San-na Fe,' the giant Indian said, comprehending the Spanish nameplace.

The shaman and the big Indian stood there awkwardly while Sister St Agnes prayed over Sister Ruth's body. Every once in a while, they would glance nervously at her out of the sides of their eyes. They refused to stare directly at her. It was obvious that they were listening intently to the old nun's words. Swanson had never seen an Apache scared so badly that he could tell it. He had now. It was an amazing, incomprehensible thing.

'Go. Come here no again.'

It was the big Indian. The words had almost been a plea.

Swanson made the sign for himself and said, 'I go from here today. But I cannot promise not to return.'

'Go,' the big Indian said. He turned and grabbed the rawhide picket ropes on the horses and thrust these at Swanson.

They rode hard for the water hole, the boy up behind Swanson and the old nun astride the other pony. She rode tolerably well, another fact about her that surprised Swanson. He guessed he'd never get her and who she really was quite straight in his mind. He let his eyes drift over the sea of rough creosote and hojase bushes. He'd seen a crow shoot into the sky in fright a couple of hours earlier but nothing since, and crows are often chased from carrion by coyotes and other predators. He let his thoughts work back to the canyon and the two Apaches. He drove his heels into the horse's sides. He couldn't figure what had happened there, but he was taking no chances on the truce being only temporary. He and Sister St Agnes had worked for over two hours to bury Sister Ruth and to fashion the cross of cucharitas wood as the old nun wanted it done. Not he nor the whole Apache nation were going to rush her into leaving Sister Ruth's grave unmarked. When they had finished speaking over it, he had sensed that she still did not want to leave. He had moved her along as gently as he could.

It was strange. The two Indians had disappeared into the desert like bad dreams as soon as they had given the horses to Swanson. It was obvious they were terrified of the old nun. For some reason known only to them, they believed she possessed great powers. Swanson smiled to himself. So, he guessed, did he. He watched her now as their horses picked their separate ways between the mesquite and the stiff, dagger-like leaves of the nolina bushes. The nolinas were in flower and beautiful. Prettier than its bigger cousin, the yucca. He studied her face. She looked shrivelled and tired. She was deep in her own contemplations, staring, without seeing, at the neck of the horse she rode. As he watched her, he realized he felt a protectiveness for her that he had never felt for anyone before. And for the first time since he was eight, there was someone who cared about him. It was a good feeling.

A blacktail jack rabbit bolted out of a stand of waxplant and darted in its stiff gait under the nose of her horse, causing the animal to shy and sidestep. If she noticed, she did not show it. The afternoon was a sweat'er. Somewhere off to their left a magpie jay made its shrill whistling call. Swanson tensed. Of all the birds in the desert, the magpie's call was the worst to try and figure the authenticity of. It was simply the most unmusical sounding call of any bird. Half the magpies he'd ever heard didn't sound like magpies. He checked the cap on the Hawken and then reined his horse to the left and made a wide sweep. He could find no tracks cutting in to where they rode. It must have been the real thing. He returned to the old nun. If she had known he had left, she didn't show it.

Swanson rode on daydreaming about California, his cattle and his fruit. He rode feeling the reality of survival sinking slowly into his consciousness. The boy clung to his back. He didn't try to talk to him.

Swanson had been pushing them hard for close to four hours now. He could tell that the boy was asleep behind him, but still hung on gamely. The sun was gone and the late evening threw a tangle of blue-black shadows on to the sand. He stopped in a gravelly stretch of dry wash that was lined with fremont phacelia to check his back trail. The horses had walked through the fremont and he could smell its skunky odour. He turned the animal he was riding around and glassed the desert behind him with his telescope. Nothing. Off to the left rose a dust devil, but there was no pursuit. They had made it. They were free. He took little bits of that thought into his mind to digest it the same way that he took little swallows of water when too much would kill him. He simply wasn't ready to handle the whole thing. He had let go of too much back there in the mountains facing the .44. It would take him some time to collect them again and put them back where they belonged. When he did, he would really know that he was free.

The horses were tossing their heads wildly and dancing. The scent of water was in the air.

Swanson left the nun and the boy holding the animals in a gully a few hundred yards from the water hole. He took his crossbow and started out across the darkening sands to scout for trail signs. The vegetation was thicker here, brittle bush, cat's-claw, and the silvery, sweet-smelling foliage of arrowweed. Big-thorn acacia trees were also in abundance and their shadowy forms made him jumpy. Some lumpy-looking mountains, a dusty brown in colour, rose above the brush-covered desert a mile or two to the north. He was moving through heavy brush when he heard a stick break and he crouched where he stood. Slowly he eased himself into the side of a creosote bush and slipped a quarrel into the crossbow. The area directly in front of him was flat and barren, and a snowy whiteness lay on the sand in a thin layer of alkali. The noise had come from the brush on the far side of the salt flat. He could see the bushes moving. It was a fair-sized animal. Perhaps a wild horse or burro . . . or perhaps a man. He waited, his eyes wide to take in the fast-disappearing light. The massive spiralled horns of the desert bighorn showed first. Swanson let his breath out in relief and then sent the bolt into the animal's skull, killing it instantly. It was a gorgeous creature, three feet high and weighing a good two hundred and fifty pounds. He took the best parts of the meat and wrapped them in the raw skin and moved off. He went slowly, studying the ground, listening for long periods to the birds around the water. With relief, he found the tracks of the nuns' wagons. He could see where Sister Elizabeth had stopped in the brush a hundred yards from the water, and then got down and scouted the area on foot. She was a smart one.

When he returned to the horses, the old nun was talking to the boy. They were both sitting on the sand in front of the horses.

'The sisters and the kids made it.'

The old nun's face lit up, her eyes disappearing in the deep wrinkles of her skin. 'That's the best news.'

A few moments later, she looked at him with a warm smile on her face and said, 'You did it, Mr Swanson. You did what God asked of you.'

He didn't answer.

Swanson was feeling well out of harm's way. Nevertheless, he was a cautious man and he made their night camp as if they were being pursued by a thousand Apache. He didn't know any other way. The water hole was in a small depression filled with rock and banked by higher sand dunes. It was the rock basin that kept the water so clean. He stood on the highest mound of sand holding the Hawken in the crook of his arm while the boy and the old nun drank and then washed their faces. A mosquito hummed around his head. He brushed it away. The twilight air was cooler. It was as beautiful a spot in this country as he had ever seen. He could smell desert lavender and hear the hum of the last bees of the day. Still, it wasn't California.

After Sister St Agnes and the boy had finished, he led each horse down to the water's edge by following a strip of rough gravel which would hide their tracks. When they were full and bloated, he led them away from the water for a long way through deep sand that wouldn't show footprints, finally walking them down into a small pocket gully lined at the ridges with pipe organ cactus.

Swanson dug the fire hole a few feet into the side of the sandy walls of the gully, then he spread a canvas over yucca stakes, awning-like, so that even looking down into the gully from a few feet away, it was almost impossible to see the fire. He could not stop the wonderful smell of the roasting sheep from wafting up the sides and into the warm desert night. It might carry for a half mile or so, but it would be hard to locate.

When they had finished eating, Swanson boiled water and made coffee. He had not had any in a week and it tasted good. Sister St Agnes drank one as well. Swanson offered a cup to the boy, but he didn't take it. They sat under the canvas, the fire dying slowly to rosy embers, casting a warm glow out of the bank on to them.

'I could use a smoke,' he said.

'I would enjoy one as well.'

They were all three sitting on the sand and leaning their backs against rocks. Sister St Agnes seemed more her old self.

'Still California?' she asked.

'Still California.' He waited a second and then said, 'You? You aren't quitting the convent after all you've put me through, are you?'

She smiled as she looked down at the sand where she poked with a small stick.

'Not quitting . . . but maybe not Pennsylvania.'

'Where, then?'

'Here, maybe.'

The smile left his face and he watched her to see if she was joking. She wasn't.

'Here?'

'These people could use the word of the Lord. Could use His love.'

'While I might agree Apaches need to be taught some religion, you'll get yourself killed doing it. You almost got yourself killed this time.'

She looked across the dark space of air at him. 'No, I didn't. I had you and you were sent from God.'

He didn't say anything for a long time. When he finally spoke, he was standing up and stretching. 'Well, as soon as I can get you to the ranch down the road, I'm going to California . . . so you won't have me the next time.' He picked up his pistol belt and bent and walked out from under the canvas. Millions of stars shot through the black velvet sky overhead. The moon was up. A coyote bolted along the side of the gully, stopped and stood looking back at him. Then it turned and was gone in the night.

He had picketed and hobbled the horses on a good stand of galleta grass on the west side of the gully. He stood in the shadows watching the animals graze for a few minutes before he stepped forward. As soon as he'd cleared the edge of the brush by a couple of strides, he heard the hammers on three guns cock and he froze.

'Put the pistol down slow.'

Swanson saw the beautiful pinto horse dancing where it stood among the mesquite. He had forgotten about the three men who hunted him. They had not forgotten him.

His good hand was raised and he tried to smile at Sister St Agnes as he came walking down into the gully. The men rode their horses behind him. The boy's eyes widened, but the old nun showed no emotion.

'Problem, gentlemen?'

'No problem, ma'am, just this feller here bushwhacked a friend of ours.'

'Doesn't sound much like him,' she said.

'Well, we've been tracking him for two weeks, ma'am, so we know we got the right man.' They were young, maybe in their late twenties and thirties, lean and tough-looking men but not riffraff. They were hard, but like most men on the frontier they respected women, and a nun was in a special class.

Sister St Agnes stirred the fire and put on fresh wood and the pot of coffee. Then she skewered a large piece of sheep and put it over one end of the fire.

'You gentlemen must be tired and hungry. We've got some fresh meat and fixings and a hot pot of coffee for you. Why don't you get down and stretch?'

Two of the riders dismounted, pistols in their hands,

and picketed their horses down the gully a few yards. The third, a thick-chested man with a beard and a wild cast to his eyes, stayed atop his horse, leaning on his saddlehorn, his pistol pointed directly at Swanson.

'This man a friend of yours?' he asked.

Sister St Agnes stopped what she was doing, looked at the man and said, 'Much more than a friend, sir. The man you're holding that gun on saved my life, saved the life of Matthew here, the lives of two other nuns and five other children. And he risked his own life desperately to do it.' She turned back to the fire. 'You'll see that he's been wounded three times. He stood off thirty Apache Indians to save us.'

Swanson didn't like being talked over like he was a horse for sale. He moved his head so that he could take in the man on the horse and the two behind him. The odds weren't good for a break. Not now.

'Thirty Apaches, heh?' The man on the horse gave Swanson another appraisal. There was no admiration in the glance, simply respect for a man who could fight that well. He would also remember to watch Swanson all the more carefully. He motioned at him to sit down in the sand. One of the two other men came behind him and tried to pull his broken arm behind his back to tie it. Swanson whirled around where he sat.

'His arm is broken, gentlemen. I set it myself,' Sister St Agnes said.

The man on the horse nodded at the other two. They sat a few feet behind Swanson, their hats off and their pistols ready. The man on the horse got down.

Matthew had stood when the men had grabbed Swanson and he was holding the pocket knife in his hand and looking at the men. Swanson shook his head, no, and the boy hobbled off a few feet and sat in the shadows.

'What did you say he did, again?' Sister St Agnes asked.

'Killed a friend of ours in Texas.'

'What for?'

'A woman.'

'Whose?'

He hesitated a few seconds. 'I guess you could say anybody's, ma'am, if you know what I mean.' The man was embarrassed.

'I do,' Sister St Agnes said, pouring coffee into the boiling water of the pot. 'How do you like your coffee?'

'Standing on its hind legs.' The men laughed.

'You say Mr Swanson bushwhacked your friend. That means, I think, to shoot someone from hiding, in the back. Am I correct?'

'That's right, ma'am.'

One of the two sitting behind Swanson said, 'He followed Brady – that was our friend – into a dark alley beside the saloon and shot him there in the back.'

'And you have witnesses?'

'Folks saw him running from the alley. And we tracked him from the hitching post where his mule was tied all the way to here.'

'Then you saw the Apaches?'

'We did. We figured they'd do the job for us. But we was wrong.'

One of the two men behind Swanson coughed uncomfortably. 'We didn't know you and the boy were down there or we'd have lent a hand.'

'I'm sure you would have. Mr Swanson did.'

'With all respect, ma'am, that don't change what he did to Brady.'

Sister St Agnes was a good cook and the meal was hot and delicious. The coffee the same. It was prime frontier fare, wild sheep roasted rare, red beans and rice with some sweet-tasting fresh bulbs of desert hyacinth that the Indians called grass-nuts. The three men wolfed it down and then looked apologetic and wiped their mouths with their bandanas. The meal and the coffee relaxed them some, but they still sat two behind Swanson, their pistols ready.

The big man fought down a burp, then excused himself. 'I ain't had cooking like that in a long time. Thank you.'

'You're welcome.' She turned to Swanson. He was sitting cross-legged on the sand watching the man to his right. 'Mr Swanson, you've heard what these men have said. What do you say?'

The night air was chill now. A soft breeze was coming north across the desert and dropping down gently on the gully. The canvas over their heads flapped. Swanson was thinking of California again, and the dog. He looked at Sister St Agnes. He didn't want to explain. That wasn't his way. They weren't going to listen anyway. But he decided to do it for her. He didn't want her thinking he was a bushwacker.

'He followed me out of the saloon. He wanted the woman. She had come to talk to me. He was drunk. He was feeling raw because she'd left his table and come to talk to me. He wanted the fight. And it was a fair one . . . excepting he was drunk. But I couldn't stop it. I killed him in a fair fight.'

'Bull,' the big man said.

Swanson's eyes and those of the old nun stayed locked until she turned and walked away into the shadows. Swanson felt bad. He knew how she felt about killings.

'Bull,' the man said again. 'If you killed Brady fair, how come he was shot in the back?'

'I shot him twice. The first one took him high in the left shoulder and he spun around when the second shot hit him.'

'There weren't two shots in him. Just one . . . square in the back.'

'There were two,' Swanson said, his voice matter-of-fact.

'Bull.'

'Jerry,' one of the men behind Swanson said, 'there was a bullet crease on the top of Brady's left shoulder.'

'Well, that could explain it.' It was Sister St Agnes' voice. She was standing somewhere off in the shadows, probably praying, he figured, for their dead friend when she ought to be praying for him. He shook his head.

There was no give in the big man. 'Bull,' he said, again, his voice fixed and final. There was no mistaking the sound.

Sister St Agnes ignored him. 'So let's say that Mr Swanson is telling the truth. You can either let him go here or we can go into Santa Fe together and tell the story to the territorial authorities there. Which would you rather do, gentlemen?'

There was silence for a long time. The wind had whipped up some and sand blew on to Swanson. Then it died completely and the quiet of the place rested heavy on them all. It was the big man who spoke for them.

'Ma'am, we respect you. We do. And we understand you don't believe in killing. We also understand how you feel about this man saving you and the boy and the others. But the fact still remains, he killed Brady. And Brady was a friend of ours.'

'He killed Mr Brady in a fair fight.'

'So says he.'

'So we ride together to Santa Fe and let him tell his story there.'

'We ain't known in Santa Fe, ma'am. It'll just be our word against his. And you'll be vouching for him. That won't work.'

'So what do you want to do? Ride to Texas?'

'No, ma'am. We're going to hang him here. Like we promised Brady we would.'

The words seemed to float over the gully like a dark cloud. Swanson had known from the beginning what they were going to do. He figured the old nun had guessed it, too. He couldn't see her standing in the dark, outside the small pie-shape of light cast out of the sandy bank by the fire. He was just as glad.

'No,' she said, her voice sounding closer. 'That's not right. You can't kill this man.'

'We know how you—'

The man's words seemed to have been torn off at his teeth. Swanson looked at him, he was staring open-mouthed into the shadows. Swanson followed his gaze to where Sister St Agnes stood holding the Hawken levelled on the man they called Jerry. The boy was standing next to her, Swanson's heavy knife in his clenched fist.

'Gentlemen, please put your pistols down on the ground in front of you,' Sister St Agnes said.

They pulled their pistols slowly, calculating whether the old nun would really fire at them. The man called Jerry pulled his last. Swanson had figured them right all along. They were decent men. There was no way they were going to draw on a woman, a nun at that.

Swanson gathered up the weapons and put them in Sister St Agnes' travelling bag. She sat on it while he went to get his horse. He had never saddled a pony as fast before in his life. The horse sucked in wind and he kneed it a couple of times until it let the air out and he was able to cinch it tight.

Swanson sat on his horse watching the old nun. She was smiling up at him, her eyes glistening. He fought the same feeling.

'You sure you'll be okay?'

'Absolutely. These gentlemen and I get along fine. And they're good men. They'll see me to the fort.'

Swanson glanced around for the boy. 'Where's Matt?'

'I think it's hard for him to say goodbye. That's all. I'll tell him you asked for him. He'll like that.'

'You take care now.'

'You do the same. And Mr Swanson, you have that talk with God. He's looking forward to it.'

Swanson sat looking down at her longer than he should have, and he had to clear his throat a couple of times before he could speak.

'It's a promise.'

He looked down at the three men. They didn't seem angry. Perhaps they were glad the old nun had stopped them from doing something they would have had to ride with for the rest of their lives. They weren't cold-blooded killers. They were simply men who stood up for friendship.

'It was a fair fight.' He turned his horse and put his heels gently into its flanks. At the top of the gully, he stopped and looked back. The old nun was watching him. Then he felt a pull on his buckskin leggings and he saw Matthew's tear-streaked face.

'Taake meee weeth yoouu.'

The boy raised both his arms to Swanson. Things seemed to flood in on him. He could see little Anna, the dog, the old nun, the vision Sister St Agnes had given him of his mother, Joshua. The boy stretched his arms harder. Swanson caught a wrist and swung him up behind. Then he turned and looked at her. She smiled. They rode. He could hear her voice as the horse picked its way carefully through the darkness along the top of the gully.

'You boys like to play cards? Good. Then come closer. Do you have any Scotch? Bourbon will do fine. While we play, I'm going to tell you about that man you just let go . . . I'm going to tell you about a miracle.'

Matthew held on tight.